THE LAST

The members of the first expedition from Mars did not expect to find survivors on Earth two thousand years after the series of catastrophes which resulted in the destruction of Luna and the partial devastation of the Earth. The situation was emotionally disturbing and politically and physically dangerous. It was made even more explosive by the actions of one man, a terrestrial 'savage', and one woman, a Martian psychologist.

by the same author

The Uncertain Midnight
All Fools' Day
A Far Sunset
Five to Twelve
Sea-Horse in the Sky

and available in Hodder Paperbacks

The Last Continent

Edmund Cooper

HODDER PAPERBACKS

Printed in Great Britain
for Hodder Paperbacks, Ltd.,
St. Paul's House, Warwick Lane, London, E.C.4,
by Richard Clay (The Chaucer Press), Ltd.,
Bungay, Suffolk

ISBN 0 340 15091 2

By A.D. 3991, the earth's magnetic field may have substantially disappeared. The result, some scientists think, could be catastrophic mutation of plant and animal life and widespread climatic changes.

For 500 years before A.D. 3991 and for as long as 2,000 years afterward, the scientists estimate, the field will be so weak that it will not trap high-velocity electrons and protons streaming towards the earth from the sun. Instead of being confined by the magnetic lines of force to the Van Allen radiation belt, many of these particles will penetrate the atmosphere and strike the surface of the earth—causing an increase in mutation rates at best, eradicating entire species of animals and plants at worst.

Time, March 15, 1968

No man is an Island, entire of itself;
every man is a piece of the Continent,
a part of the main.

JOHN DONNE

It was high noon. The old man lay sprawled against the trunk of the tree, getting what shade he could from the dead branches. All around was an almost featureless plain whose only contours were small boulders and outcrops of rock half covered by drifting sand. The old man gazed vacantly at the rough wooden hand-cart that contained his few possessions. He had come a long way, but he didn't have much farther to go. He knew it.

A rattlesnake, the only other living creature in the vicinity, lay coiled no more than a couple of metres from the old man. It regarded him with vague tolerance. The old man was too weary to want to kill it. The rattlesnake was too sick to want to strike. Together they savoured the comradeship of despair.

Presently, the old man recovered himself sufficiently to be able to stand up. He lurched towards the cart and groped among its contents. With a sigh of satisfaction, he found a small leather-faced box, one side of which revealed a recessed glass-covered screen.

He took the veecorder back to his bit of shade and fell in a heap. When he had recovered from the exertion, he looked to see if he had annoyed the rattlesnake. He hadn't. There was, apparently, this understanding between them.

He fumbled with the veecorder. The replay stud didn't work too well these days, and the micropile was low. Still, hopefully, it would last him out. He shivered again and felt the piece of bone discreetly poking through the shrivelled flesh on his chest. Yes, definitely, the veecorder would last him out.

He wondered why he had been doomed to live so long. Probably it was some kind of judgement. If, indeed, there was anyone or anything to judge.

The veecorder contained only one cassette of tape. It had been played many times. Too many times. There were defects in both sound and vision. But they were no problem. The old man knew every syllable, every gesture, every pattern of light and shade by heart.

"See, rattlesnake," said the old man with difficulty. "I'll show you how it was once. I'll show you how the end began and how the beginning ended. I'll show you it took only an ounce of titanium to cut down the hope of mankind."

He pressed the replay stud. Nothing happened. He pressed the stud again and nothing happened. He shook the box and tried once more. Still nothing happened.

The rattlesnake appeared sceptical.

"Confrick it!" rasped the old man. "Confrick it!"

He hit the box and was rewarded with a low electronic whistle.

"Ha!" he said triumphantly. The rattlesnake remained unconvinced.

But after a moment or two, the screen began to glow. The picture stabilized, and a man in a null G bubble that seemed to be hovering high above a swarm of ants said brightly: "Lo, folks. As predicted, Kennedy Ground is filled full of those who have come to hear the word of the prophet. So let's flip to E level and find out what that voice of our times, Thomas Mulvaney, has to offer this noble throng."

Cut to a close-up full face of Thomas Mulvaney, a magnificent seven-foot negro with eyes of fire and features that would have grossed a billion for any old-time big shot in Hollywood U.S.A.

"Friends," said Thomas Mulvaney, in a voice rich with sincerity and passion, "brothers, sisters, children. Our forefathers were slaves, our grandfathers were second class citizens. This we know. This we remember. But we—we are the salt of the earth. We who were oppressed are now free. We who were weak —and I mean only weak politically—are now strong. We lift up our heads. We carry ourselves high with pride. We are the living force of man. Tell me, brothers and sisters, what are we?"

Cut to the multitude, and thunder rolling from half a million throats. "We are the living force of man."

"We are the future," roared Thomas Mulvaney. "Tell me, brothers and sisters, what are we?"

Again the thunder. Again the affirmation.

"Our brother, the white man, has conceded our right to live," went on Thomas Mulvaney. "Our brother, the white man, had to concede our right to live—because he did not wish to perish."

"Yea! Yea!"

"Our brother concedes us the right to walk the Earth—a world which he has already over-exploited—while he soars out into space. I ask you a question, my dear family. I ask you a question! How many of us are there in Space Station Seven? How many of us are there in Luna City? How many of us have jetted for the bright new lands of Mars? The white man, our brother, has given us only the freedom of Earth, has he not?"

"Yea! Yea!"

"No, you are wrong, my generous people. The white man, our brother, our cunning brother, has not given us the freedom of Earth. We took it. But then the white man, our oh-so-clever brother, saw that the game was not yet lost. He looked up to the stars. He vaulted across the firmament, seeking new fortresses, new bastions, impregnable to those whose blood is red but whose skins are dark. I ask you a question, my loved ones, I ask you a question. How shall we gain the freedom of space?"

"We shall take it," said the thunder. "We shall take it ourselves."

It was then that the assassin's bullet struck.

The old man switched off the veecorder as that magnificent black body convulsed among a crop of microphones like a spent scarecrow in a field of metallic corn. The old man didn't want to see any more. It hurt too much. Besides, he had already seen it too many times.

The sun beat down as if it was determined to fry all living things. The old man shaded his eyes and looked across the arid plain towards the horizon. He thought he could see a highway and trees in the distance. He even allowed himself to think that he could see buildings and hear the vague murmur of a great city. Then, after a moment or two, he killed the luxury—because luxuries should not be enjoyed too much. And because there was nothing there.

He turned to the rattlesnake.

"Rattlesnake," he said, "that Thomas Mulvaney was a strong man, full of fire. Not a good man, maybe. Not a bad man, maybe. But somebody you felt you had to listen to. Somebody you felt you had to understand. He didn't make no trouble, mind. Well, not big trouble. He just picked it up when somebody else left it lying around . . . Guess that's how he earned his ounce of titanium . . ."

He broke off for a moment or two, wiped the sweat from his forehead and gazed vacantly around. Then he recollected that he was giving the rattlesnake a history lesson.

"You wouldn't believe how much death there is in an ounce of titanium," he went on. "You wouldn't think there was enough to go round. Not for all of us! But there was, rattlesnake. Hell, there was. I'm telling you."

The rattlesnake raised its head a little, but offered no comment.

"They gave Thomas Mulvaney a fine funeral, a real fine funeral. There was white men even that jetted half round the world to sing the twenty-third psalm. They gave him a fine funeral, and then they set up the Thomas Mulvaney Space Foundation. And then the Power Men moved in. Them Power Men! They weren't anybody's people. They moved in so quietly nobody knew they was there . . . And then a whole lot of negroes were trained for space. But mostly, they weren't just negroes. Not just people. They were the special ones. They were the Power Men. And when there was enough of them in the Station, and enough on Luna and maybe enough on Mars— well, I guess that ounce of titanium just got tired of waiting . . . So they tried to take over the Station, and they took over on Luna and maybe they even took over on Mars. And then they talked to all the folks—black and white—down here on this old green ball. They said: 'People, we got buttons, and we got missiles, and we're up here and you're down there. So listen hard.' "

The old man sighed. "Well, I guess nobody likes that kind of talk . . . So that's why there ain't no more Station and no more Luna in the sky and why the green Earth is just yellow and dry and empty. And that's why there's just you and me here, rattlesnake, talking some about that powerful ounce of titanium."

The old man lost his balance and fell over. The rattlesnake rattled fitfully but without conviction. The old man picked himself up again with difficulty, and scratched the bone poking through his chest. He scratched agonizingly because it itched, because it hurt and because it felt very hot. Then he fumbled in his pocket.

"See here," he said to the rattlesnake. "This piece of metal is a rare item. It's worth ten thousand years of history. Look at it good."

The bullet was scratched and misshapen. He tossed it at the rattlesnake, who received it without resentment.

The old man turned to his veecorder once more. This time, he got it going first try.

"Friends," said Thomas Mulvaney, in a voice rich with sincerity and passion, "brothers, sisters, children. Our forefathers were slaves, our grandfathers were second class citizens. This we know. This we remember. But we—we are the salt of the earth . . ."

Tears were running down the old man's cheeks, leaking precious moisture from his spent body.

He looked at the handsome face on that small screen, and murmured softly: "My son! Oh, my son!"

CHAPTER ONE

Kymri walked through the jewelled forest, exulting in a young man's pilgrimage to nowhere. He was happy and miserable; and he thought he was sick. Because he was seeing everything as if for the first time. He did not care that he was alone. He did not care that Noi Lantis was many kaymets away. He did not care that the king might enquire for him or that someone else might lie between Yosseline's legs this night. He cared only that he should enjoy his elsdykik while it lasted.

Occasionally, he prayed to Godfred for spiritual guidance. He received none, and was almost relieved.

The forest was green with life and wet with the promise of more life. The fine rain clung to his cloak of firebird feathers, as if enmeshing it in a web of crystals. The leather triangles of manhood slapped damply against his buttocks and his groin. Steam occasionally rose from the blade of his spear, and his sandals drew a soggy music from the living earth.

Monkeys chattered, birds protested and lianas bound the earth to the misty sky. The forest was emerald, beautiful. In the early morning it was a steam-bath of creation.

Suddenly, Kymri heard the great noise again. But this time he was awake and could not ascribe it to some prank of Godfred. The noise was real; and it was thunder yet it was not thunder. It was the greatest noise he had ever heard.

It tore through the air like a knife. It hit him and made him wince with pain. It destroyed the squabbles of monkeys and birds, and made the forest wail with terror. It was the thunder of death, or the thunder of eternal life. Or both.

Kymri stood still and looked up, straining to see through the green roof of trees and the grey veil of the sky. There was nothing.

Sometimes the sky was blue, but rarely. Sometimes the rain stopped, but rarely. Sometimes at night the veil was drawn away to reveal the burning intensity of the stars. The priests said that the stars were other worlds, that each star was a furnace in the void, providing the warmth of life for other forests, other kingdoms, other men . . .

The noise died. Kymri began to breathe once more. Presently the forest shrugged off its fear and was as it always was.

He sat down on the trunk of a fallen tree and tried to think about his problem. Whether to endure castration for the sake of knowledge or retain his manhood and for ever be denied access to the lore of generators, wire messages, anodynes and curatives.

The tree-springer, looped high above him, thought that he was not aware of its presence. Kymri, his mind not on his problem, thought that the tree-springer was ready to drop. He guessed right.

As the powerful beast fell, its compact but heavy body ready to crush anything that breathed, Kymri sprang sideways. Disdaining the spear, he sprang back as the great weight hit the earth. With perfect timing, he delivered the stamp of oblivion, feeling a satisfying crunch as his heel struck the unprotected base of the creature's head.

He stood clear as the dead thing, not knowing it was already dead, thrashed and contorted, blindly seeking vengeance. It was a pity that the tree-springer was too heavy to drag back to Noi

Lantis. Its armoured body would have earned him much kamen, and not only with the women.

But Kymri's regret was short-lived. For before the tree-springer was still the noise came back. Only this time it was louder. So loud that he fell to the ground, covering his head and ears, yet still screaming with the pain. It was so loud that surely it must fill the world and, by its very intensity, break all living things asunder.

Just as Kymri, realizing he could stand the torture no more, groped for his spear, the thunder that was not thunder became transformed into a roar—as of mighty waters falling from a great height.

He looked up, and saw fire in the sky. White fire, yellow fire, blue fire. Diamonds of fire dancing among the tree-tops, shrivelling the foliage, scorching the forest.

Surely, the elsdykik had gone too far. Surely he was being punished for his idiocy. Surely the end of the world had come.

But before he could take the final dive into a pool of madness, the roaring stopped. And he was left numbed. With a dead tree-springer and with the scent of burning in his nostrils.

CHAPTER TWO

The outward jump was over, and history had been made. The outward jump was over—it had taken seventy-three days—and back home the trivees would be pouring forth millions of D shots of this poor, parched, battered, worn-out planet in millions of homes. The Administration would be happy because it had guessed right, and the pure Vaneyites would be happy because their anticipations were justified. So all would be well in the world of the free.

Mirlena sprawled in a contour pod on the navigation deck and stared up through a plastiglass panel at the stars. Practically everyone else was in the saloon whooping it up. The ship was in a two-hour orbit, and before long there would be another of those agonizing sunrises. But there was still a little time to lounge in a contour pod one thousand miles above the nightside of the planet and contemplate the infinite sadness of life.

Mirlena was afraid of the stars. She had always been afraid of them. They were a visual representation of all that was unknown and unknowable. They supplied a disturbing perspective. They continued to burn indifferently through all the agonies of man. They were burning pin-points of detachment. They were the cold clear eyes of a cosmic perspective.

"Dr. Stroza, are you here? Dr. Stroza, where are you?"

She identified the voice instantly. It belonged to Rudlan Others, the Senior Communications Officer. She had made love with Rudlan many times; but outside the G bunk—or, more correctly, when others might be present—he always called her Dr. Stroza.

"Well, Rudlan. What takes you away from the party?"

He switched on the blue light, and the stars dimmed. "People are missing you. They say: what has happened to our lovely psychologist? They say: why does she not grace us with her erotic splendour and drink all the cycloids under the table?"

Rudlan's voice was firm and musical and very attractive. It was his greatest asset. In the dark ecstasy of love, it made him seem as tall as the Red Range, as warm as the Broken Lake. Interesting how, in romanticism, she used geophysical similes . . . In reality, Rudlan was small, neat and plus-feminine oriented . . .

She was annoyed with him for switching on the blue light and breaking the spell. "Nothing has happened to the less-than-lovely large-breasted psychologist whose alcohol quotient exceeds her intelligence quotient by twenty points. Except that she was enjoying solitude—now, unhappily, disturbed."

"My love," said Rudlan, "you are in a state. Come and get outside three iced redballs with speed. It will solve your equation."

Mirlena laughed. "Psychologist, heal thyself? Sorry to disappoint you, Rudlan, but there is no equation. It was a time for solitude, that is all. Even a psychologist must be allowed to dream."

"Then don't dream too much, clever one. Vaneyism is as strong on this ship as ever it was back home. The P.O. has a file on you, and he transmits more code groups than anyone else in this vessel."

Again she laughed. "The Political Officer is a failed Lothario.

Possibly, he radios back for advice."

"I'm not joking, Mirlena. Your absence is noted. Kord Vengel may be, as you say, a failed Lothario. But he is a vindictive man. He sees shadows where none exist."

Mirlena sighed. "So I must come to the party."

"I think so . . . But what is so wrong with a party to celebrate a successful jump of forty million miles? Here we are, on the first large deep-space flight for many years. It is something to celebrate."

"It would be something to celebrate," she retorted, "but for the people and the motivation . . . But, as you say, we must allay fears of anti-Vaneyism. So lead me to the iced redballs, Rudlan, and guess who I will sleep with tonight."

"Do you want to be on the touch-down sloop?"

"You have guessed right, comrade."

"Then you had better sleep with me—because I have been required to submit a possibles list to the captain."

Mirlena lay back in the contour pod. "Love now and receive payment later?"

"I'll do my best," said Rudlan as he lowered himself beside her. "You're a strange woman—even for a psychologist."

"Goodbye, stars," murmured Mirlena, closing her eyes. "Goodbye, my bright enemies . . . Stick to the essentials, Rudlan, or both our absences will be noted."

CHAPTER THREE

It was a long time before Kymri recovered from his fear. He lay on the ground, quivering, trying not to whimper, while the scent of burning drifted down to his nostrils. Presently, he dared to look up; and was relieved to find that the diamonds of fire had gone. There was nothing now but smoke and steam among the scorched tree-tops. The forest knew well how to deal with fire—the forest and the eternal rain.

The head of the dead tree-springer lay close to him. Its black reptilian eyes seemed to stare at him reproachfully. Suddenly, Kymri was ashamed that he had met death only with death. He had been aware of its presence, and he could have moved before its slow mind came to the inevitable conclusion that food offered was not food to be refused. He could have moved and so have avoided the encounter, and so have avoided the death of the tree-springer. But pride in himself had made him stay—the destructive pride that would one day cause him to accept a challenge that he was not capable of meeting.

The priests were right. There was not enough humility in his soul for him to pursue knowledge for its own sake. Therefore no castration and no initiation into the mysteries of electrics and alchemy and medicine. He was born a commoner and a commoner he would remain.

He thought of the thunder of Godfred—for what else could it be?—and of the strange fire that had opened the sky almost above his head.

Godfred was the divine joker; but surely this joke contained too much of terror and little of laughter. According to the scripture, there had once been great beasts that could assume the shapes of birds roaming the sky. According to the scripture, these creatures had ravened upon cities, gorging themselves while at the same time excreting thunder and fire and death. In those far off days—before the founding of Noi Lantis, according to the legends—there had once been many cities. But the great beasts had destroyed all the cities, until there was nothing left for them to feed upon. And so they also encompassed their own destruction.

But what if one of the creatures still survived? What if the last of the monsters, dropping thunder and fire in its wake, was intent upon seeking out Noi Lantis and indulging in a final orgy? Kymri shivered at the thought. It was absurd but—but the thunder had beaten him to the ground and the smell of fire was still in his nostrils.

He knew not what to think. He knew not what to do. Now the wretched pride was eating him again. He was afraid of being afraid.

He looked up once more and saw what he had previously not noticed—that the fire trail ran in a straight line across the tree-tops. Follow the trail, Kymri told himself, and you will arrive either at the end or the beginning. Follow the trail, and you follow the path of the sky monster—if, indeed, there is such a thing as a sky monster. And if there is not, why, there will still be a story worth telling when the cups are filled in the evening.

Will it be called Kymri and the Sky Beast or Kymri and the Thunder of Godfred?

Amused by his own childishness, Kymri picked up his spear

and let his trained forest eyes decide in which direction the diamonds of flame had moved. Presently, to confirm his deductions, he climbed a small red-fruit tree as far as the first scorch marks, to discover which side of the tree had been seared most. Pleased that his judgement had proved right, he continued to follow the trail of withered tree-tops.

He did not have to travel far, nor did he experience any difficulty. For as he walked along, it became evident that the path of fire had bitten deeper and deeper into the forest.

Presently, he found himself in a place where the sky fire had reached down to the very earth, blackening the entire trunks of trees and burning everything that had once lived on what was now a circle of dead earth, wide as a temple games ring.

Smoke still rose from the ground and the charred trees nearby; smoke and steam, swirling slowly upwards against the fine rain. Tears came to Kymri's eyes, and he choked on the acrid, sickening smell of all the burnt greenness.

Had he then arrived at the sky-beast's lair? Would the creature, disturbed, suddenly come upon him and consume him in one hungry gout of liquid fire?

Oddly, curiosity was greater than fear. He did not want to flee. He wanted only to find out. But smoke and steam filled the air, and the nauseating smell and the dying heat were too much for him.

He knew he was going to be sick, and he thought it better to be sick at a distance. He managed to hold back the disagreeable impulse until, half-blinded, he had stumbled in retreat for about fifty paces.

By the time he had disposed of the unsettled contents of his stomach, the remaining smoke and steam had almost dissipated. He returned to the circle of dead earth, amazed at what he saw in its centre.

For there, standing on three mighty legs, each twice the height of a man, was a great black sphere which still hissed and spat and steamed where the rain touched it.

CHAPTER FOUR

Streven Luse, chief officer, pressed a stud on his desk console and swung round in his chair so that his back was to Mirlena. The shield panel slid away and the observation panel revealed a massive orange and red glare, with thin straggles of blue near to the twilight zone. The face of the planet was blank, tantalizing. It was a face of heat and hunger and deadness, relieved only by a dazzling carpet of mist over the south polar region.

"There will be hazards—very serious hazards, I think," said Captain Luse. "I do not wish to risk more personnel than are strictly necessary. Why, Dr. Stroza? Why do you have this compulsion to be among the first party?"

Mirlena tried to keep the excitement out of her voice. "I was appointed ship psychologist," she said flatly. "It seems logical to me that I should be with the landing party."

"There will be no intelligent life for you to practice your psychology on. And while it is true that the unmanned probe has reported oxygen rich atmosphere and minimal radio-activity, I must remind you that the sheer physical strain of landing on a three G planet is not to be endured lightly. That is why the party has to consist of my best men."

Mirlena shrugged, although the shrug was unnoticed. "I was not hoping to practice my psychology, as you put it, upon the natives," she retorted. "It is my business to observe the crew in stress conditions. This is a stress condition. Therefore I should be present. As far as the physical aspects are concerned, may I remind you, Captain Luse, that all of us have undergone the same training, conditioning and surgery. Like you and everyone else here, I have lived for months in lead-lined suits so that my new muscles could adjust to the strain placed upon them. Any of us on this expedition could win any event of the Lympiks back home. We have adjusted to the three G problem." She laughed. "In fact, we have become so adjusted that our bodies, deprived of multi-G stress, seek compensation in other ways, as you know."

Captain Luse swivelled back to face her once more. "Mirlena, let's not play games. Let us understand each other clearly. The reasons are not physical." Streven Luse was a mature, intelligent man. He had the look of one who wished to say more than he felt he should.

Mirlena thought for a moment. Then she said quietly: "Is your cabin tapped?"

He looked shocked. "I should hope not! Who would dare—"

"The Political Officer would dare anything," she interrupted, "if he thought it would provide a return on investment. Surely, Streven, you have lived with Kord Vengel long enough to know what he is like?"

Captain Luse smiled. "The lean and hungry look?"

She nodded. "Such men are dangerous . . . But suppose I were to assure you—are you certain this place is clean?"

"Quite clean. My god-like role as captain has not diminished a certain facility with electronics . . . I take the trouble as a matter of routine. You would be surprised at some of the things I hear. Much could be made of them at a Vaney tribunal."

"I like you, Streven. You are a straightforward man."

"I like you, too, Mirlena. You are a very complicated woman. But there is still the question of Vengel. He gives you a political

25

B rating."

She laughed. "In return for the Stability C I gave him, and because I did not welcome his intrusion in my sleeping cycle . . . I assume he has approved himself as a member of the touch-down crew?"

"You assume correctly."

"But suppose I were to assure you—"

"You said that before."

"Suppose I were to assure you that within the next few hours he will develop high temperature, fever and hallucinations?"

Captain Luse raised an eyebrow. "I hope the implication is only that you are clairvoyant."

"What else? But, of course, one meets fire with fire. And if Kord Vengel is ill, then it follows that he will not be able to touch down."

"So?"

"So a substitute will be needed."

"I see. And who should the substitute be, do you think?"

"As I have already said, it is my business to observe people in stress conditions."

Streven Luse was silent for a while. Then he said: "Tell me, Dr. Stroza, how long do you think the Political Officer is likely to be ill?"

"Four days, five days. A great deal will depend upon his metabolism—and, of course, the efficiency with which his sickness is treated."

"You can—how shall I put it—arrange these matters?"

"Yes, I think—putting it somewhat carefully—I can predict with some certainty."

Captain Luse swung his chair round to stare at the planet once more. "We have discovered so much about this place already. It depresses me. I cannot understand why you have to be one of those who feels the very deadness."

Mirlena, having achieved her victory, stood up. "Because I have a weakness for graveyards," she said. She turned to go, then stopped and added inscrutably: "And because two thousand years is a very long time."

CHAPTER FIVE

Kymri crouched, holding his spear tightly and regarding the sky beast with apprehension. Would it discharge thunder and fire at him, annihilating him with its searing breath? Or would it at any moment rise deafeningly into the sky to continue its quest for Noi Lantis?

The sky beast moved. It put forth strange limbs and rotated them slowly. It opened glassy eyes and glared blankly at the forest.

Kymri, afraid to stay and afraid to run, tried to convince himself that he knew how to die. But the sky beast seemed indifferent to his presence. He continued to live. And think.

And he thought: The death of a man is a small price to pay for the life of a city . . . I wish I were older . . . I wish I had known more women . . . I wish I had been castrated so that I might dwell upon the mysteries of generators . . . I wish this was only the dream of a drunken elsdykik . . . I wish I were elsewhere . . . But the death of a man is a small price . . . Now, if I can but aim true, and the spear penetrates an eye, surely the beast will perish?

Suddenly, all his doubts and fears were resolved. Suddenly, he made up his mind. He stood up and shouted the ancient battle cry of the temple athletes: "Strength in water!"

Then, expertly, he hurled his spear, falling to the ground as soon as he had done so, closing his eyes and covering his head with his hands against the anticipated anger of the sky beast.

He had aimed well. He was rewarded by the sound of something breaking. Presently, amazed to find that he was not dead and that the sky beast had not retaliated, he dared to lift his head and look. The blade of the spear had penetrated the creature's eye. The shaft hung loosely from the black sphere. But even as he looked, another eye opened.

Still the creature did not retaliate.

Kymri began to feel oddly humiliated by his own continued existence. Realizing joyfully that he had at last received the greatly prized death wish, he sprang to his feet, uttered the temple cry once more, and took a running leap at the great black sphere. In mid-air, he snatched the spear free from the blinded eye and fell in a heap under the creature's body and between its mighty legs. He thrust violently upwards with the spear, seeking the creature's soft parts.

There were no soft parts. Metal struck metal, and the sound and the feel of it were unnerving.

Kymri panicked, running from underneath the creature, darting first this way then that way, to escape the terrible forces that must surely consume him.

Nothing happened.

Thirty paces from the sky beast, he fell down and sobbed with terror.

Still nothing happened.

He remembered his manhood, picked himself up, and hurled the spear once more. Again he had hurled truly. Again there was the breaking sound as another of the strange eyes shattered.

No vengeance?

No vengeance!

Kymri was baffled. But from his very perplexity he somehow

28

derived courage. Another running jump, and he snatched the spear away once more. This time he did not grovel. He got out from under the sky beast and looked for more eyes. He found four.

He destroyed four. But when he had destroyed the last one, the creature put out two more slender limbs.

They were too slender to hurl a spear at. Filled with the death wish, Kymri squatted by the very legs of the sky beast and looked up at its thin, tantalizing arms. He doubted that he could hit them with the spear. But . . . But might he not climb up the legs of this strangely somnolent metal beast and render the arms useless in some way—perhaps even wrench them off?

Kymri began to laugh. Not only did he have the death wish, but Godfred had afflicted him with divine madness also. Here he was, a young man of Noi Lantis, armed only with a light spear, pitting himself against a metal monster that doubtless contained beneath its impenetrable skin such secrets and energies as only Godfred might know.

Indeed, perhaps the monster was not a sky beast but Godfred himself, deriving much amusement from one of his subtle jokes.

"Monster!" shouted Kymri defiantly. "Are you Godfred?"

There was no response, though one of the metal arms seemed to quiver slightly.

"Monster!" shouted Kymri again. "Are you alive or dead? It is I, Kymri op Kymriso, who ask the question. I, Kymri, who have put out your eyes."

The creature seemed totally indifferent both to his questions and to the injuries it had received. Perhaps it was dying. Perhaps it was already dead. Thus encouraging himself, Kymri took off his cloak and began to climb one of the metal legs as if he were going up a hairnut tree. The legs were still warm, uncomfortably warm. It hurt him to have to grip them so tightly.

He reached the sphere, but his hands could find no further purchase. The nearest metal arm protruded from the sphere at a distance farther than he could stretch. But he might just be able to leap and snatch it as he fell.

He tried, and was lucky.

Or unlucky.

The metal arm was flexible. Further, it had not been designed to sustain the weight of a man. It bent under his weight, then was ripped from the sphere, trailing socket and connections after it.

Kymri found himself swinging down to the ground, his aching hands still tightly gripping the arm. As he fell, he experienced a further sensation of triumph. Bit by bit, he was surely destroying that which had seared the forest as it journeyed to seek out the city.

His triumph was short-lived.

No sooner did his feet touch the still steaming earth than it seemed as if a great hammer was simultaneously striking every fibre of his being. The jolting, shuddering pain danced up and down his arms, jerked his limbs convulsively and made him dance grotesquely and agonizingly.

He could not let go. No matter how hard he tried, he could not let go. He uttered a terrible scream and hung semi-conscious from the thin metal arm. Mercifully, several connections were broken by his agonized dance. The arm came completely free of the sphere.

And Kymri fell limply to the warm wet earth.

CHAPTER SIX

"So the probe is dead," said Captain Luse. "Have you any theories?"

Rudlan Others looked uncomfortable. The theory he was about to propose went against all the evidence, and against all accepted notions of the planet. Quite possibly it was an anti-Vaney idea, and as such could get him into serious trouble.

"The lenses were destroyed one by one," said the Communications Officer.

"So?"

"So there could be a pattern in the attack."

"Why do you call it an attack?" demanded the captain sharply.

Rudlan Others floundered. "Partly because of the regularity with which the cameras went out of action and partly because the odds are against successive failure in a series of independent systems."

"Who was monitoring?"

"Sir, I was."

"You saw nothing?"

"Well, sir . . ."

"Out with it, man."

"The visibility was very poor. Rain and steam, sir. One could not expect much penetration or definition so soon after touchdown."

"What in the name of Vaney did you see?"

"It—it," Rudlan Others could not bring himself to give an accurate definition, "it looked like the face of a ghost, sir."

"A ghost? Dammit, man, there are no ghosts! Can you be more specific?"

"I—I don't think so, sir." Rudlan Others was sweating. Captain Luse was a reasonable man, but the interview was going just as badly as he had feared. "Of course," he added hopefully, "it could be a trick of the light—or even an odd configuration of vapours."

"I see. You taped, of course."

"Yes, sir. Standard procedure."

"Then show me this ghost," said Captain Luse drily. "Show me the departed spirit that has cost us one of our two independent probes."

"Would you like to come to the Communications Room and see it on the large screen, or shall I have the playback piped to this office?"

"I like my ghosts large," said Captain Luse drily. "We will go to C.R." He stood up. "I must warn you that, as the officer responsible for this breakdown, you will have to justify the failure not only to me but to those who have placed great reliance on your ability. You will recall that the crew of this vessel were chosen from an élite. You will also recall that much has been invested in the project. I am answerable for any weakness or mistake, and all in this vessel are answerable to me."

"Yes, Captain Luse," agreed Rudlan Others miserably. "But may I remind you, sir that I did not design the probe's communication system."

They left the captain's quarters and went to the Communications Room, where they saw the brief playback. Camera one supplied a hazy view of a tropical rain forest. So did cameras two and three. So did camera four—except for the ghost image. A brief, hazy moment. A humanoid outline. A lightness. A sudden blur—and then nothing.

"Again," said Captain Luse. But the playback left him no wiser. Like Rudlan Others, he did not wish to see what he thought he might have seen.

"Your ghost," said Captain Luse at length, "is a creature of steam." He laughed bitterly. "Hot air, sir, and the presence of water vapour."

"Yes, Captain Luse."

"Dr. Stroza will explain the psychological mechanism, no doubt."

"Yes, sir."

"I shall require a more coherent explanation of the breakdown in communications . . . Possibly, the probe touched down in a swampy area and unfortunately sank . . . You understand?"

"Yes, sir."

"There is no intelligent life form on this planet," said Captain Luse. "Our previous investigations have demonstrated that that basic theory is sound."

"Yes, sir."

"On the other hand," went on Captain Luse, "I do not propose to waste any more time. Neither do I wish to hazard our second probe. These one-way jobs are pretty useless, anyhow. Besides, we already have enough data for our requirements. So the manned touch-down will take place as scheduled . . . Can you give me the exact location of the dead probe?"

"Yes, sir."

"Good. I think we should get as near as possible . . . One likes to be tidy about these things. But, rest assured, there are no ghosts, nor are there intelligent life-forms."

"No, sir."

"One other thing," said Captain Luse. "You are in charge of logistics, are you not?"

"Yes, sir."

"Then kindly provide light defensive weapons for the landing party."

CHAPTER SEVEN

The stiffness brought him pain, and the pain brought him awareness. Opening his eyes, Kymri did not at first know where he
was. Nor did he remember what had happened. But then he
discovered that he was lying under the impregnable belly of the
sky beast; and the memories and the fear returned.

He lay there for a few moments, not moving, believing that
the sky beast believed him to be dead. There was no movement
above. No eyes observed him. Experimentally, he moved an arm
—and was not annihilated. He gained confidence. Perhaps the
sky beast, too, had been sleeping. Or perhaps that last agonizing
encounter had been the monster's death throe.

Surreptitiously, Kymri stretched his limbs. The effort caused
him some anguish. There were burn marks on his hands; and he
could not understand how he had gained them.

Presently, he felt well enough to attempt to escape. He was
sufficiently astute to realize that, though the creature had not
moved, it might still harbour some dreadful surprises inside its
strange body. Besides, the fact that it still stood upon its mighty

34

legs was an indication that life persisted. Therefore his escape must be conducted with great speed.

He was much afraid; but there was little to be gained by dwelling upon the fear. Endeavouring to put all thought from his head, Kymri lurched to his feet and half-ran, half-hobbled from under the dreadful creature. He had not travelled more than six paces when his legs gave way and he fell in a heap. Anticipating instant death, he was amazed once more when nothing happened. He dared to glance at the sky creature. It was bleak, black, immobile, silent. Surely it was dead.

He stood up. Nothing happened.

He retreated slowly. Still nothing happened.

He advanced. Again there was no reaction. Clearly, then, he was the victor. Singlehanded he had destroyed this monster that was many times the size of a man.

Kymri was filled with joy and pride. He made so bold as to walk up to the body and slap the rigid legs with his hands. He shouted defiance at the beast. Then he began to compose in his head the story that would be told in Noi Lantis. Obviously, the story would have to be verified. Obviously, there would be an expedition from Noi Lantis for that very purpose. Kymri pictured himself standing proudly by the dead creature as he received the plaudits of the multitude.

A thought suddenly struck him. He did not know how long he had slept. He looked up through the scarred green roof of the forest and was amazed to see blue sky. It had stopped raining; and the sun climbed low above the edge of morning.

Therefore his fatigue/sleep/unconsciousness had lasted at least one night. He recognized now the weakness that had caused his legs to buckle as he ran from under the sky creature. It was nothing to do with pain or the stress of conflict. It was simple hunger. He was so hungry that the very thought of food brought a sweat to his forehead.

He lurched unsteadily away from the dead sky creature in pursuit of food. It did not take him long to find it; for the forest abounded in food of one kind or another. He did not want meat —in any case, he had no means of cooking it—so he went in search of ground pears, which were easy to eat and gave almost as much strength to a man as meat or cheese. He did not find any ripe ground pears, since the fruit was popular with many creatures of the forest, and others had ravaged the pear clumps before him. But he did discover the nest of a Lancer bird. It contained three large eggs. He stole one and retreated hastily before the female returned to sit. Even if he was in the best of condition—and he was not—Kymri would have been reluctant to match himself against the speed, agility and ferocity of a disturbed Lancer. They were among the fastest ground creatures in the forest; and their long sharp beaks had been known to penetrate metal armour.

For reasons that he did not understand, Kymri returned with his egg breakfast to the corpse of the sky beast. He squatted at the perimeter of the circle of blackened earth, expertly cut off the crown of the Lancer egg with his spear and proceeded to dispose of the contents. Fortunately the egg was not very old, and the chick had hardly begun to form.

As he half-chewed, half-drank the viscous fluid, Kymri kept a watchful eye on the strange form of the sky beast and began to consider the sequence of events that had transformed his elsdykik into a nightmare. He could make no sense out of them. Necessarily, the beast must be one of those referred to in the scripture; for no one of Noi Lantis had seen such a thing in generations. Indeed, Kymri was not even sure that anyone who had ever lived in Noi Lantis had seen one at all. Such beasts belonged to prehistory, to the legendary days when many cities flourished in lands more distant than the mind of man could imagine.

Presently Kymri began to dwell upon the nature of the beast itself. There were two things—two important things among many—that really puzzled him. The first was its symmetry. No truly living creature, in his experience, possessed such symmetry. A man—a great craftsman—might create a perfect sphere and set it pleasingly upon three legs; but Nature would not. As the priests said, it was man's duty to care for form and Nature's task to care for function. Therefore, since it was not asymmetrical, there was much that was unnatural about the beast. Further, there was the question of its skin.

Undoubtedly, the skin was metal. Nature could not create in metal: that was the province of man. But what kind of man, what kind of priest could conceive and fashion a monster such as this? And if, indeed, there were such a man, such a tower of strength and skill and learning, who could create a great being that rode the sky with fire, was that being a living thing or merely an extension of its creator's mind? A machine?

Kymri's head ached. He felt a whole cloud of crazy thoughts flapping around inside it like demented butterflies. The questions he asked himself, the thoughts he thought were truly incomprehensible. Better to leave such debate to the priests and the wise ones.

They, at least, would be able to determine whether the sky beast was man-made or one of that ancient self-creating breed that had once fed upon cities far beyond the sunrise and the sunset. Perhaps, truly, it was the last of such monsters. Perhaps the last sky beast had been seeking the last city; and it had been granted to him, Kymri, to destroy it before it could destroy.

He smiled to himself. Such a story would be worthy of an entire temple wall. It would be remembered as long as Noi Lantis stood.

Please, Godfred, he pleaded silently, let the sky beast be a sky beast and let it be the last of the sky beasts. Thus will I, Kymri, achieve greatness in the eyes of my people.

But, instantly, he knew that it had been a terrible mistake to appeal to Godfred, for Godfred was the divine joker. And the terrible joke was not yet over.

There was a great crack as of mountains parting.

The forest trembled, the ground quivered, the air screamed.

Kymri held his head and screamed also as great diamonds of fire danced high above the forest, searing the blue sky and putting forth a great whiplash of heat.

It was all happening again. It was all happening more terribly even than before.

It was madness without the release of death. It was unbearable.

Kymri lost consciousness as he tried, vainly and grotesquely, to wriggle himself into the very earth like a frenzied worm.

CHAPTER EIGHT

The sloop had touched down remarkably close to the dead probe —far closer indeed than Rudlan Others had expected. Along with Mirlena and the three other members of the crew, he waited patiently inside the small exploratory vessel while radiac and atmosphere tests were automatically carried out by the sloop's own probe system.

Mirlena was feeling rather pleased with herself. Kord Vengel had succumbed to a somewhat mysterious ailment exactly as she had predicted, and was at this very moment simultaneously being tranquillized and further weakened by regular doses of a somewhat powerful anti-biotic. When the Political Officer became coherent again, he would no doubt cogitate upon the strange illness that, after weeks of excellent health, had frustrated his plans to be among the first party to touch down on the dying planet. He would also, no doubt, meditate upon the fact that his replacement in the landing team happened to be Dr. Stroza, his prime suspect for deviationism.

But, Mirlena told herself, there would be time enough to worry about that later. Kord Vengel had already demonstrated that, as far as the overall mental health of the expedition was concerned, he himself was a serious psychological hazard. The man's incipient paranoia was getting on everyone's nerves. He saw conspiracy, malice and deviation where none existed. He was not so much a spy as a provocative agent of discord. Who, then, would worry if he met with a simple accident?

Mirlena checked her own paranoid impulse sharply. To dispose of Kord Vengel—a task that could easily be accomplished—would be to set herself up as judge, jury and executioner. Not only was it unethical, it was psychologically dangerous. If one once crossed the great divide between rational opposition and irrational liquidation, there was no telling where the process would end.

Anyway she refused to think too much about Kord Vengel. She could not allow anxiety and insecurity to inhibit the elation and the sense of achievement she felt now that the sloop had landed.

She looked at her companions—all men—and experienced a sense of comradeship, a feeling of group identity. Before the sloop had left the parent vessel, back in the two-hour orbit, Captain Luse had jokingly referred to the touch-down crew as a bunch of grave-robbers. Well, grave-robbers they might be. But was there not danger and excitement—and even dignity—in robbing the tomb of kings?

And that, despite her knowledge of history, her education and her political conditioning, was how Mirlena regarded this planet. As a tomb of kings. Throughout her life, it had been no more really than a tragic and tantalizing legend, distorted by Vaneyism and corrupted by the sheer passage of time.

But now the planet was real, and she was real. And soon she would walk upon its enigmatic surface.

She looked at the silvered regulation space suit that she wore, and tried to visualize it as a suit of armour that might have been worn upon this very world several millennia ago. It would be pleasing to bring a touch of life to a dead planet. It would be pleasing to let ghosts ride upon the wind.

She looked at her companions and wondered if they were as impatient as she was to get outside the air-lock.

Meiron Menders, a likeable and incredibly young physicist, was busy checking the data output concerning the sloop's immediate environment. Tam Mbela biologist, white-haired and comfortingly stolid, had glued himself to the manual periscope and, drunk with discovery, was giving a running commentary to no one in particular about all he could see. Actually he could see very little, since the heat and steam of arrival had yet to disperse. Jol Quhern, engineer and navigator, a little wizened robot of a man, was totally unconcerned by the fact that his name would now endure for generations. He was too busy closing down pile temperatures and calculating feed fuel consumption. And Rudlan Others—dear, ineffectual Rudlan—was talking back to base in precise clipped words, feeding Streven Luse with information as emotively as a Black Hills housewife might list her laundry items. Pretty soon, Rudlan would be relieved of his onerous task; for base would pass over the horizon, thus giving Rudlan a respite for at least ninety minutes.

"Radiac and atmos the anticipated norm," announced Meiron to no one in particular. "Oxygen slightly higher than we thought. But it's good to get a little drunk once in a while. External temperature nineteen point five. So we shouldn't cook too much unless we start running . . . I think I'm going to wear it."

"The greenery!" exclaimed Tam. "By crippity, I've never seen so much—at least, not outside the Blue River Glass. It's quite fantastic. If this is a dead planet, I'll—" he stopped, abashed.

Rudlan signed off, and heaved a sigh of relief. "Thank Vaney for that. The Cap is burning himself blue that he didn't come on the first drop . . . What greenery? We blackened it."

"No we didn't," said Tam ecstatically. "We made a tiny hole in a great green sea. This is a rain forest we're in. Three days from now, you won't be able to find a sign of touch-down. The soil is so much alive, you can hear it singing."

Rudlan shrugged. "Oxygen narcosis," he said drily. "Anticipatory oxygen narcosis. Tam can't wait to get pissed."

41

"When do we get outside?" demanded Mirlena. "Surely somebody can tell me that? I've been waiting for this moment for about ten centuries."

"As far as I'm concerned," said Meiron, "you can go right now. The tubes will still be hot, but you can get clear of them pretty quickly. They will cool down fairly soon . . . Who is going to be first through the lock?"

"Ah, yes," said Tam eagerly. "May I point out that the immediate biological conditions seem to indicate that it would be appropriate if I—"

"No, you may not," retorted Rudlan. He looked at Mirlena. "We are four men and one woman. It looks to me that if Mirlena wishes to exercise her prerogative . . ."

"Thank you," said Mirlena softly. "I would like very much to be the first. But I am not going to trade upon my sex. I suggest we draw lots."

"Count me out," said Jol Quhern, looking up from his knee-pad. "I still have a few sums to do. And when the mix chamber is cool enough, I want to go down and see why the reaction rhythm was uneven. We had to compensate with a plus zero five thrust."

"No lots," said Rudlan. "I vote for Mirlena." He smiled at her. "Interest upon capital invested."

"Push her into the lock," said Meiron impatiently, "otherwise we shall all sit here mouthing irrelevancies."

Mirlena did not need to be prodded. She slipped herself expertly into the tiny air-lock, closed the door and equalized with external pressure. When the go signal appeared on the panel, she opened the external door and threw out the flexible ladder. After a final check on the locking gear of her head-piece, she climbed carefully down the ladder and set foot upon the scorched ground.

The feeling of exhilaration was immense, unbalancing. She wanted to laugh, to cry, to sing, to dance. Instead of which, she moved quickly but carefully away from the hot tubes of the sloop, gazing in rapture at the steaming green wall of vegetation that confronted her.

Presently, she was followed by Tam Mbela and Rudlan Others. Last of all came Meiron Menders, who almost fell down the last few rungs in his excitement.

Then the four silver-suited invaders began cautiously to explore the world they had waited so long to see.

CHAPTER NINE

Kymri returned simultaneously to consciousness and hysteria. It would happen again. It would always happen again. Throughout the rest of eternity there would be fire in the sky, thunder in the forest, and that searing, tearing pain of unendurable vibrations that drove him past madness and into oblivion.

It would happen again. It would happen again and again. This was neither life nor death but a nightmare to which there could be no end.

He wept and held himself tightly, digging his fingers angrily into his own arms, ashamed of his weakness. He sat on his haunches, crying and rocking to and fro like an old woman keening for the dead.

Time passed. He spent himself in the effort required to express his fear and misery. Time passed; and at last the shame was stronger than the misery or the fear.

He was doomed, and he knew that he was doomed. The knowledge served to restore his pride. For there was nothing else to lose. Except, perhaps, his sanity. And under the circumstances, did that matter?

He wiped the sweat and the tears and the soil from his face, and stood up. He found his spear and his cloak. He looked at the dead sky beast.

"So your brothers seek to avenge you, monster," he shouted. "Let them come, I say. I do not doubt the reckoning. But know that Kymri op Kymriso will not disgrace his people. We are of flesh, and you are of metal and fire. But these things, also, can die—as I have seen. So let them come . . . And if this be a prank of Godfred, let him come also. For there can be little glory in the destruction of so small a thing as a man."

Kymri felt better. The sound of his own voice had cheered him. Though his spirit was weak, the words were brave. It was as if someone else had spoken them. As if, in the strange radiance of the death wish, Kymri had drawn strength from nowhere.

He looked around him. The forest was quiet once more. There were no monsters near. They had not yet sought him out. Therefore, as a hero of old, he would go forth to meet them.

He tried to remember the death song he had learned as a child. But the words were embedded in the sticky blackness of his thoughts. Therefore he extemporized, feeling drunker than drunk on this, the darkest elsdykik of all.

"Kymri, son of Kymriso," he sang.
"Kymri of Noi Lantis, having seen much,
    desires nothing more
    than to die with grace, occasioning
    a smile on the face of Godfred
    and the discomfiture of his enemies.
    Kymri op Kymriso is the singer.
    Let there be greatness in his song."

As he walked and sang, he felt better and better. He felt implacable and as invincible as Godfred. He felt he could knock trees down with his hands and strike dragons with a look. Truly, the death wish was a great art form. The pity—trivial thought—was that none survived it.

He was totally unprepared for his next encounter.

For two reasons.

The first because he had never seen a ghost, and the second because he had never seen a silver ghost.

There it was, no more than thirty paces away, dancing.

He crouched, wondering if a spear thrust could dispose of a silver ghost. Somehow, he thought not. And, in a way, he was amused. He had been expecting more sky beasts. But, such are the whims of Godfred . . .

He crouched—and almost fell over, as he saw the ghost remove its crystal head. Beneath the crystal, there was blackness. But the blackness was alive.

He shouted. In fear and defiance, he shouted. The silver body and the blackness above it turned towards him. He discerned eyes. He discerned eyes, wide and terrible.

Almost relieved that he had at last found death, he ran to meet it. He ran towards the terrible creature with spear arm raised and the temple cry upon his lips.

Death moved slightly, raising a silvered arm. There was a pricking sensation in Kymri's chest, but he did not heed it. Death moved again, and there was another slight feeling of being pricked.

He saw the black face that was strangely beautiful. Even as he fell, aware of a sudden freezing lethargy in his limbs, he noted the black skin and the black hair of this silver embodiment of death.

His spear plunged into the ground almost at the feet of the first black-skinned woman that Kymri had ever seen.

CHAPTER TEN

Mirlena looked down in awe at the temporarily paralysed body of the first living white man she had encountered. Then she drew back suddenly, crouching, with the anagun ready in one hand and an optic bomb ready in the other. It was possible that the savage who had tried to kill her with his spear was not alone. Even now his companions might be stealthily encircling her.

She regretted wandering off on her own. The sloop was not far away. Nor, presumably, were Rudlan and the rest. If she called, no doubt they would come. But if there were many of these primitive people around—and, for all she knew, they might possess more formidable weapons than spears—the result could be disastrous. Streven Luse could not afford the destruction either of the touch-down party or the sloop that had brought them. Besides, there was the question of pride. How stupid and how weakly feminine she would look if she called for help and there was nothing to fear.

The radio was in her headpiece. The headpiece lay on the

ground, not far from the savage, where she had dropped it in surprise. Better to wait a little and see what happened. Surely the anagun and an optic bomb would hold off any attackers until she could be reinforced? Rudlan, she knew, had a sweep rifle; and Tam Mbela carried an assortment of small, noxious, chemical weapons. The three of them with their sophisticated weapons would surely be more than a match for an entire regiment of savages such as the one that had fallen to her stun darts. And, of course, there was Meiron as well.

Mirlena was amused by her own rationalizations. So this was what happened to some people under stress. They dithered uncertainly—secure in the belief that they were evaluating real or imagined threats and planning accordingly.

Time passed. She stared at the green curtain of the forest and saw nothing. Time passed, and she became sure that the young man—for, demonstrably, he was a young man—that she had hit with paralysis darts was alone.

She put the optic bomb in a pocket of her space suit, picked up the headpiece she had dropped, and went to inspect her victim. She could hear voices. The general receive channel was open. She could hear Meiron Menders chattering away excitedly. He had found the dead probe and was inspecting the damage. The sound of a familiar voice steadied her. She was in control of herself once more.

The young man in his cloak of crumpled feathers lay sprawled on his face. Gently, Mirlena turned him over. The white face was pinched and drawn. The eyes, dark and uncomprehending, were still open and, presumably, still registered whatever was in their field of vision. The mouth sagged a little, revealing a fine set of teeth. The nose was sharp, and so was the bridge of the nose—harsh, but not entirely displeasing, although totally unlike the classic negroid features that were the aesthetic norm. She looked at the eyes once more, and experienced pity for what she thought she saw in them. She wondered what, if anything, this poor immobilized savage could be thinking.

Suddenly, Mirlena became aware of the enormity of her discovery. It had been predicted that, as far as intelligent life was concerned, the planet was dead. It had been claimed that the sins of the white man had been visited biologically upon each degenerate and successive generation until the white side of the human race had vanished.

Yet here was a perfect specimen. True, he was primitive. But physically he seemed perfect. No abnormalities. Limbs, hands, feet, body, head, features all acceptable—apart from the disturbing whiteness. So much for Vaneyism. So much for dogma. When the news got back home it would trigger a political explosion.

Mirlena's exultation was short lived. She tried to think herself into being Kord Vengel, the Political Officer. How would he react to this discovery that homo sapiens, white, still persisted? Kord was a one-hundred proof fanatic—a pure Vaneyite, for whom any modification of basic theory was nothing less than heresy.

If the facts did not fit the theory, Kord Vengel would be quite prepared to change the facts. Back home, he was a man of considerable influence; and it would be easy enough for him to get the necessary authority to declare a Jehad upon these unlucky indigenes who accidentally challenged the almighty word of Vaney.

Mirlena was frightened. On behalf of a race she did not know, she was frightened. What would Vengel call it—a sanitation job?

At least, he would need a little time. Streven would not consent to a liquidation programme unless it was backed by the highest authority at home. Eventually, it would be . . . Unless . . . Unless it could be demonstrated that these white survivors were not the kind of homicidal, xenophobic megalomaniacs that Vaneyism decreed they should be.

"Poor savage," said Mirlena softly to the man lying motionless at her feet. "Poor sad little savage. We have a hard task before us, you and I. We have to prove that you and your kind have a culture that is worthy of survival. We have to prove that you belong to a stable and industrious race, with no dreams of conquest, with no mad longings for domination . . . You saw me, and your first reaction was to hurl a spear. It's going to be a hard task, little one . . . It is difficult enough for my own people to understand that all blood is red, so how difficult will it be for you?"

She took Kymri's spear out of the ground where it had fallen. She examined the blade and the shaft carefully. Then, with a dexterous movement, she snapped the spear in two.

Deliberately she broke it in his field of vision. Perhaps he could not see it, being still unable to focus properly. But she thought she detected a momentary flash of anger in his eyes.

CHAPTER ELEVEN

There were dreams, nightmares. Some were terrible, some merely incomprehensible. Such was the pleasure of Godfred . . .

He could not move. Sometimes he could not even think. Sometimes he was rational enough to know that he was insane.

Black faces swam about him, supported by bodies of silver. Silver arms touched him, prodded him, explored his body. He was lifted and carried; and the trees of the forest danced above his frozen eyes, and the silver ghosts made noises to each other. And the noises had meaning and no meaning, for the words were all wrong.

Kymri had a thought. It was a good thought. He thought that he might swallow his tongue and die. But his tongue was frozen in his mouth, and his arms were frozen to his body. Somewhere, Godfred must be laughing fit to weep.

Now there was no more forest above him. Only a strange dull whiteness. And lamps. Electrics, of course. One was an arm's length from his nose. It glowed with a dull, blue-white coldness, hypnotizing him.

Suddenly, there was a great noise. No, not a noise, a shaking. No, not a shaking, a noise. A noise and a shaking.

Two men sat on Kymri's chest. But they were invisible. He could not breathe. His ears were singing, his head was bursting, darkness rippled over him in waves.

It lasted a long time. Agony is always a long time. Fear makes it longer.

A black face loomed over him. Somebody or something was lifting his head. Then his head was encased in crystal; and the voices and the noise were cut off. He wanted to hear again—anything. Thunder, strange voices, the sounds of the forest—anything. But he was encased in silence, and there was only the feel of a strange garment that now enclosed him totally.

The invisible men were no longer sitting on his chest. Now he was full of langour, floating euphorically down the river of death. There was no weight to him any more. He had only to will it, and he would soar and hover like a bird. He had only to will it, but he had no will power left. Because he was floating down the river of death; and a man does not challenge the very nature of things.

Kymri tried to make peace with himself and with his memories. He thought of childhood. Childhood in Noi Lantis had been pleasant. There had been bad times; but it was the good that were worth remembering. He thought of the market place shortly after dawn. He smelled the smell of new-baked bread, and cooked meats sliced so thin that you could see the light through them. He thought of the first girl he had ever discovered—as a girl. Norvane was her name. Or was it? It didn't matter. What mattered was that she had removed from his eyes the child's film of blindness. He had seen what beauty was and could be. He had seen a woman disguised as a girl, a girl disguised as a woman. He had seen and touched breasts that were magically small, yet large enough to shake thunder out of his ribs. He had kissed lips like none that had ever been or ever would be. His flesh had been moved, and her flesh had been moved. And there had been few words but much enchantment.

Afterwards, they had met many times. But one day she did

not come. Many days he waited for her by the pool where they had first loved and that, by the virtue of that love, belonged to them alone. She came no more. He never knew what had happened to her, but prayed always that it was something good. Or, at least, quick. Peace, Norvane! I, Kymri, have also completed my journey.

But in that he was mistaken. Kymri had not completed his journey. Indeed, he had only begun it.

When the sloop matched orbital velocity with its mother vessel, the complex docking operation began. Presently, he was transferred to the hospital cabin of the mother vessel. Presently, his space suit was removed. Presently, the paralysis wore off.

Presently, he, a white native of Earth, found himself heavily involved in the task of trying to communicate with a black Martian.

CHAPTER TWELVE

Kymri was not allowed to stay in the hospital cabin very long. Kord Vengel saw to that. He had recovered from the mysterious fever that had prevented him from being among the first landing party, and seemed to realize vaguely that he had been the victim of a conspiracy. So, for several days he took malicious pleasure in being as obstructive as possible to everyone—including Captain Luse—while remaining technically within his rights.

But most of all he concentrated his attention on Mirlena and on what he referred to as the 'obsolete animal' she had encountered on the dying planet of Earth. It was sadly obvious that the planet could no longer be classified as dead. But at least it could be re-classified as moribund, which was practically the same thing.

In a way, Kord Vengel was even glad that basic theory would have to be temporarily modified. No doubt this would eventually provide him with an opportunity for political action. He relished the prospect of being able at a later date to order the extermination of all such obsolete animals that could be found.

Mars would not tolerate this unhappy reminder of the Dark Ages. Whatever anyone else might think, these regressive white creatures were doomed.

Meanwhile, Mirlena felt that she had won a battle if not a war. The battle was for Kymri's immediate survival. Marsbase decreed that he should be studied physically and psychologically, and that attempts at communication should be made.

At the same time, the Political Officer insisted on Kymri's removal from the hospital cabin to the cage. The cage was no more than a small box with bars, scarcely the height of a man, that had been welded into a convenient bulkhead recess in the stores section of the vessel. It had been constructed in case there was any animal life worth transporting back to Mars for adaptation and exploitation. It was a small cage because there was not a great deal of space available for such facilities and also because no one expected to find any animal life of any size or significance still existing on a planet that, by all the laws, ought to be dead.

Kord Vengel had emphatically reminded Captain Luse of the treacherous and homicidal habits of the white races. Streven Luse could not afford to take risks or to make mistakes. Therefore he had ordered that the obsolete animal be locked up and that no one—including Dr. Stroza—should enter the cage unaccompanied.

Mirlena had protested violently, knowing that under such conditions it would be very hard indeed to win the confidence of and establish communication with a primitive man who had been snatched out of his natural environment and plunged into what, for him, must be a nightmare existence. But her protests were ignored; and so any investigations she wished to conduct had to be carried out in spite of the formidable psychological barriers of imprisonment.

Fortunately for her, when the terror and trauma of recent experience had worn off a little, Kymri also became interested in the possibility of investigation. If he were not dead or insane, if what had happened to him had been deliberately arranged by Godfred, why then he wished to know as much as possible about the joke—so that he could savour it more fully.

His clothes had been taken away—the sadly tattered cloak of firebird feathers and the leather triangles of manhood—and he now wore the one-piece shipboard suit that was commonly worn by the members of the Martian expedition. He hated the touch of the synthetic material and the horrible feeling of being totally enclosed. He thought of tearing it off; but then he did not wish to appear naked before his enemies. Besides, it was possible that the garment might enable him to conceal some weapon that he could eventually use either to escape or to inflict some damage before he was killed. That he would be killed in the end, he did not doubt. Which was another excellent reason for learning more about this prank of Godfred. If a man has to die, reasoned Kymri, he may perhaps die with better composure if he can understand the nature of his passing.

Synthetic gravity bothered him. The ship developed a syn G field only about one tenth that of Earth. It was quite strong enough to keep the Martians happy, but it posed some problems for the simpleton from Earth. However, after he had knocked himself unconscious once or twice by moving too rapidly and with too much spring in his step, Kymri got the hang of it. He imagined that he was light as in water, and adjusted his movements accordingly.

But where—oh, where—were the rain, the sun, the forest and all that he knew and loved? Here was nothing but warm air, strange food, black faces, silver covered bodies and intense loneliness.

At first, many black faces swam about on the other side of the metal bars. There was much talk in a language that was alien and yet, somehow, he felt he ought to understand.

Gradually, he began to recognize the most frequent visitor. Was it not the one who had plunged ice into his limbs in the forest? The one who had shamed him by breaking his spear as he lay helpless?

The creature's voice was soft. It spoke to him regularly in the words that were so near meaning, and yet so far from it. He asked many questions, hoping that his words would prove to have more meaning for the alien than the other words had for him. When he spoke, he noticed that the creature manipulated some kind of machine. Once, when he had stopped speaking, he heard his own words come back to him from the machine. And was terrified.

Then the alien smiled and caused the machine to spew forth alien words. Kymri, hating this creature, smiled also; for mixed with the hate there was fascination. Also, there was the sure knowledge that this one was a female of her kind.

The silver suit could not disguise the female shape; and since those other black-faced beings were fashioned as men was it not logical to assume that their women would be fashioned as women? Perhaps their faces only were black, due to some strange application or terrible exposure. Perhaps beneath those silver suits the flesh of their bodies was entirely normal.

So Kymri smiled at the female, wishing to gain her confidence if only so that she would come near enough to be killed. She clearly desired him to talk, therefore he talked greatly. But he was careful not to talk of Noi Lantis or of the strength or numbers of his people. For who could say when or if his words would take on meaning for her? So he talked chiefly of the forest and of his battle with the sky beast. It was good to speak of the death of the sky beast, for the telling restored his pride and manhood.

Strangely, what bothered him most in all these strange and terrifying experiences was the abolition of night and day. Recessed lights—electrics—glowed not too brightly in the walls of his cage. They glowed constantly, so that he did not know whether it was night or morning. This disorientation frightened him, chiefly because he had no means of assessing the length of his captivity. He felt, but did not know, that he must have endured imprisonment for many days. He counted nine meals of strange revolting food—mush that had no texture in it and need not be torn or chewed—but this made him little wiser. These black creatures might provide him with food once a day or three times a day. There was no way of telling.

Sometimes, he slept. Sometimes he dreamed. Mostly, he only half-slept, waiting for the time when his captors tired of him and he would be killed.

CHAPTER THIRTEEN

Having assured herself that there was no immediate threat to the primitive white man, Mirlena disengaged herself from the political and historical controversy that had been occasioned by her discovery. Because she had found Kymri, the primary exploration programme of the first landing party had been cut short; and the sloop was now scheduled to make a second touch down, as close to the first as possible, during the course of the next few days. But Mirlena was not even interested in that.

She was interested only in establishing real communication with the man whose very existence defied the canons of Vaneyism.

In several exhausting and emotionally charged sessions, she had managed not only to get large quantities of Kymri's speech patterns down on tape, but also to establish the meaning of a few simple nouns. Even with the small amount of knowledge she had already acquired, she had been able to detect certain similarities between Kymri's language and early period Martian. The discovery was exciting and exhilarating.

But one of the great difficulties in trying to get the key to this Earth language lay in breaking down what she had got on tape into separate words. Here she was helped by Rudlan Others who, as a communications specialist, was able to devise a simple programme for separating the words and then, with early period Martian as an experimental control matrix, run a computer programme to establish the probable value of the words used and their relationship with each other.

It was indeed a very happy accident that Mirlena had been able to establish the link with early Martian. It saved a great deal of time, for with the data derived from the early Martian language model, the ship's computer was able to print out an entire lexicon which included the probable meaning of every word that Kymri had used.

With mounting excitement, Mirlena began to interpret the tape recordings, while at the same time teaching herself to emulate the sounds that Kymri used. She gave no indication to Kymri that this was happening until she felt she was ready to converse freely with him. There were two reasons for this oddly secretive approach. The first was that she thought he would be inclined to speak less freely if he knew that she was getting a command of his language, and the other was that she wished to obtain an immediate psychological advantage as soon as she was confident that she could communicate.

She worked feverishly and with little sleep, mindful that unless she could produce some very cogent reasons not only for Kymri's continued survival but for the survival of the Earth culture he represented, time was on the side of Kord Vengel and orthodox Vaneyism. Back on Mars, mothers still frightened their children with terrible stories of the white bogeymen who had destroyed all that was good and wholesome. Back on Mars, the legendary archetypal white man was seen as a combination of Mephistopheles, Herod and Genghis Khan.

So Mirlena worked hard, hoping that once communication had been established, she would discover enough about Kymri and his tribe or nation to justify not only their reprieve but even, perhaps, some technological aid. For, however wholesome their psychological balance might prove to be, it was abundantly clear that these white survivors lived a primitive and precarious existence.

Presently, she decided that the time had come to speak to this now very dejected white savage in his own tongue. Within one hundred hours of his arrival in orbit, she had analysed his language—with Rudlan's help—and had taught herself to speak it if not quickly at least fairly accurately. It was something of an achievement.

On her way to the stores section, where Kymri was imprisoned, she encountered Kord Vengel who was evidently just returning from a visit to the cage.

Vengel, a tall graceful man, was exceptionally handsome and knew it. With bright, piercing eyes and a neatly pointed beard, he looked like an incarnation of Tom Vaney himself, the Earthbound Moses whose martyrdom had opened the way to the promised land of Mars two thousand years ago.

Kord Vengel gave Mirlena a long and searching glance. Personalities apart, he desired her hungrily and physically; and he knew that her body, if not her spirit, desired him. A man knew such things. And particularly he knew it with this woman who presumed to be more than a woman but who lacked the necessary force and ruthlessness to compete in a world of men.

"Going to see your little white pet, Mirlena? I think you will be very disappointed in him. He seems apathetic. Perhaps it is all too much for him, to be brought up from his little patch of jungle to confront the gods." He laughed. "I shouldn't be at all surprised if he doesn't die of shock."

"If that is the only threat to his life, I shall be content," said Mirlena evenly.

"You wish to preserve degeneracy, then?"

"I am not concerned with degeneracy, Kord—at least, not in the sense that you mean. I am a psychologist. It is my business to investigate people and their behaviour patterns. For me, this primitive white savage is an exciting specimen. Intensive study might reveal much, not only of his own attitudes but perhaps even of the attitudes of his ancestors."

"The ones who destroyed Earth?"

"The ones whom history tells us destroyed Earth," she answered carefully.

"I hope you will not find your specimen too exciting," he retorted. "The consequences could be dangerous."

"For me?"

"For you . . . And Mirlena, remember that before you are a psychologist you are a woman."

She moved to walk past him. "I have not forgotten it."

The corridor was narrow, and Vengel stood so that she could not squeeze past without touching him. She tried to reduce the area of contact as much as possible, but he turned and leaned hard against her, pressing her back to the steel panel.

Mirlena met his piercing gaze, and was only half-surprised by a pleasurably hateful tightening in her breasts.

He kissed her hard, and their tongues briefly explored each other. But suddenly the mist cleared and the unthinking moment of sensuality was gone.

He released her. "The other side of the coin is love," he said softly.

"No, Kord," she said, drawing away, "the dark side is only lust."

CHAPTER FOURTEEN

Kymri sat despondently on the floor of the cage. He had managed to steal a spoon of soft metal—no good as a weapon, but at least he could make marks with it and so pass the time. By continually sharpening the edge of the spoon against the bars of the cage, he could sharpen it enough to scratch a few faint lines on the metal floor.

He had already laboriously drawn the sky beast, and now he was vainly trying to amuse himself with a few simple geometrical patterns. As soon as he heard Mirlena's footsteps, he hid the spoon in one of the pockets of the shipboard suit that he was now learning to endure without too much discomfort. He stood up and turned his back to the door, thus expressing contempt for his captors.

"Good morning, Kymri," said the woman's voice softly. "I hope you will be less lonely, now that I speak your tongue."

Kymri spun round, forgetting the low field of gravity, and fell in a heap. He picked himself up cautiously. The black-faced woman smiled.

"It is difficult to remember that one is no longer heavy," she said in a not unpleasing accent. "I hope you have not hurt yourself."

"I am well enough, woman," he said coldly. He pointed to the small recorder she was carrying. "So the machine has helped you to speak my language?"

"Yes, Kymri, the machine helped. But a greater machine was needed also, and then I, too, had to do much work."

Kymri laughed, then said very haltingly in words that sounded like middle period Martian: "The white savage needs no machine."

It was Mirlena's turn to be astounded. "That was very good indeed. Has someone been teaching you?"

The effort to reply in Martian was too great for him. He relapsed into Earth language. "I thought greatly about the sounds you made, and the sounds made by the males in your hunting party. It seemed that they should have some meaning. So I remembered some of the sounds and searched through the words of my own language for the nearest sounds. Thus did I learn . . . There was nothing else to do. Also, it is good for a man to try to understand his enemies."

The interview was not going as Mirlena had planned. She had hoped to obtain a psychological advantage by talking to Kymri in his own language; yet, once he had recovered from his initial surprise, he seemed to be almost in command of the situation.

"The first thing you must understand is that we are not your enemies."

Kymri smiled. "If friends plunge ice into my limbs, destroy my weapons, strip me of my clothing and confine me in a cage such as is suitable for wild creatures of the forest, what then must I fear from my enemies?"

"We are not your enemies," she insisted. "Remember also that in the forest it was you who attacked me."

"True," he admitted. "There were reasons. I had experienced many wonders and had even defeated a sky beast. It was a time for wonders, and I thought that you were a silver ghost. Clearly it was in the nature of things that you would defend yourself."

"If I had not done so," she pointed out, "you would surely have killed me."

Kymri's eyes flashed. "It would have been fitting. First, there was the death of the sky beast . . . Whatever happens, that you cannot take from me."

Mirlena sighed. "No, we cannot take that from you. But the sky beast was not a creature of destruction, Kymri. It was a machine that we had sent to explore the forest in which you live. You destroyed our machine, and so we came to look for ourselves."

He tried to remember all that had happened. Could it be that this black-haired, black-faced woman who concealed her body and possessed great skills was telling the truth? It was a possibility. Yet the coming of the sky beast had been preceded by great thunder and fire, as in the legends. And even in defeat, it had wrought great pain in his limbs. Shuddering, he recalled how it had touched him with such agony that he had fallen unconscious beneath the dying metal body.

"The sky beast—your machine—fought terribly," he said. "Even when I had put out all its eyes, the creature stung me with its metal arm."

"I wish I could explain to you what really happened," said Mirlena. "The machine was sent down to the forest from the sky. Its task was to look at the forest—through the special eyes you destroyed—and then send pictures of what it saw to us who waited for this information far away . . . I think the sting it gave you was accidentally caused when you destroyed some of the machinery. It is what we call an electric shock."

"Electrics?" said Kymri, suddenly interested. "The machine has electrics?"

"You know about such things?" Mirlena was surprised.

"I am not ignorant," he said warily. "Much that is strange can be accomplished with electrics. Perhaps it is as you say. Now, I wish to know where I am, and why I am held in this cage. Also, I wish to know how the weight has been taken from my limbs. Further, since I am to die, I desire to know what kind of people —if, indeed, you are people—it is that can bring thunder and fire into the forest and machines that send pictures a great distance. Let us talk of these things, woman, or let us put an end to words. For I can lose nothing by remaining silent."

Mirlena regarded him with some admiration. Many terrible and inexplicable things had happened to this little white savage. Yet, despite all the trauma and his apparent conviction that he was going to be killed, he remained remarkably self-possessed. In a similar plight she wondered how she or Rudlan Others or even Streven Luse would have reacted. Not, she suspected, with quite as much dignity or courage.

"Kymri," she said, "we will talk of such matters presently. It may be that you will find it hard to understand some of what I say. But I will do my best to explain clearly. It is important to me, also, that you know as much as possible. Then, if you are satisfied, in return you shall tell me about yourself and your people. Does that seem reasonable?"

"We shall see," he answered non-committally. "Let us talk, and we shall see."

"I know your name," went on Mirlena. She smiled. "It is one of the words you used frequently when I was recording your speech patterns. So perhaps I should begin by telling you my name. It is Mirlena."

"That is all your name?"

"No. Mirlena Stroza. That is all my name."

"I am Kymri op Kymriso."

"I know. Is Kymriso the name of your father?"

He shot her a suspicious look, and hesitated before answering. "No. My father has no name . . . Stroza, this is the name of your father?"

She nodded. "And also of my mother."

"Thus do we present ourselves," he remarked obscurely. "You are truly a woman, and not some creature bearing the aspect of a woman?"

Mirlena was surprised. "I am a woman."

"Then show me your body."

Suddenly, Dr. Mirlena Stroza, psychologist, emancipated black Martian, was discomforted in the presence of a white savage. She

65

tried to analyse her own reactions. It was not that she was embarrassed or ashamed. She would not have been ashamed to take off her clothes before any man—on Mars. No, there was something odd here. Some nameless, fundamental inhibition, and a sense of danger.

Kymri sensed her perplexity, her sudden disorientation. He gripped the bars of the cage and laughed. "There is no need for fear, woman. The animal is secure within its cage."

Mirlena started. Intuitively, Kymri had sensed what was stopping her. And now she herself knew. Fear. Absurd fear. For there was obviously no reason to be afraid. She smiled grimly to herself, wondering how many generations ago it was that some anonymous negro slave had given her this legacy—an instinctive, xenophobic fear of exposing herself to a white man.

Mirlena stifled an impulse to retreat. Calmly, she unzipped her shipboard suit and held the fabric back with her hands, revealing smooth black shoulders, full firm breasts and muscular stomach.

Kymri inspected her. Contrary to her expectations, the fear did not diminish.

"So," he said casually, "you are indeed a woman, and the skin is black all over. Thank you. I did not know. Though strange, it is not entirely unpleasing . . . My body I think you have already seen."

Thankfully, Mirlena zipped up her suit. She had been sweating, and the thin material stuck to her skin. But as she covered herself, it felt comfortingly like a suit of armour.

"Yes, Kymri, I have already seen your body."

"It is fashioned in the same way as those of the males of your party?"

"Yes."

"The shape of your body is entirely familiar also." He laughed. He sat on the floor of the cage and laughed.

Mirlena, having been humiliated by an archaic fear, was now disconcerted by a total lack of comprehension.

"The thought amuses you?" she ventured.

Tears ran down Kymri's face. "It is a great joke. It is surely the best joke Godfred ever invented. Day and night are different. Yet daylight and darkness cover the same forests . . . Oh, yes, it is a great joke! Night and day are natural enemies; but the forest is what it always was."

"I—I am not sure that I understand you," said Mirlena.

He regarded her quizzically. "The forest," he explained simply, "is as the spirit of man."

CHAPTER FIFTEEN

"As Political Officer, I have a right to see every message except those sent and received by the Chief Officer." Kord Vengel was in the Communications Room, endeavouring to assert his authority with Rudlan Others. The two men disliked each other, principally because of Mirlena.

"That is normally the case," conceded Rudlan, delaying his explanation until it could achieve maximum effect. "You get your copy file regularly, Kord. I don't know why you are so steamed up . . . You don't think anyone would want to sabotage this project, do you?"

"What I think about sabotage," said Kord pointedly, "will be revealed when the time is ripe. I get the copy file, as you say. But it does not contain any messages originated by Dr. Stroza. And I happen to know that she has been sending quite a lot to Marsbase."

Rudlan smiled. "Ah, I didn't know it was Mirlena's stuff you were interested in," he said silkily. "You should have said so at first. It would have conserved our adrenalin."

"Stop playing games. I want to know why."

"Then you should have read your last file copy carefully. The Standard Procedure page has a small addition."

"Why wasn't I told?"

"It was there for you to read. In view of the importance of her present assignment, Dr. Stroza applied for and was granted a Class One security rating. She now reports and receives in cypher." Rudlan laughed. "I presume it is not wise for mere mortals to know how her investigation of the savage is progressing. After all, it may even affect the fundamental philosophy of Vaneyism. And then we should all have headaches, shouldn't we?"

"Class One security!" exclaimed Kord. "The woman is a fool. This, more than anything, is basically a political problem."

"Then someone fairly high-powered at Marsbase must also be a fool," pointed out Rudlan. "She got permission the same day of application."

Kord Vengel smiled grimly. "Dr. Stroza has a talent for doing everything the hard way."

"In which case, Kord, she has only one other rival aboard this vessel . . . Look, man, why don't you relax? We are all locked up in a tin can and we have to live with each other. Mirlena doesn't want a war on her hands—neither do any of us. But she has what she considers a unique opportunity to investigate what she grandly calls the primitive white psyche. And you keep breathing fire and doom all over her work."

Kord Vengel snorted. "Mirlena can keep her pet a little longer. But before I'm through, I'll have permission to breathe fire and doom on every white savage left on this planet. Personal memory may be short, but the racial memory is long. This creature's ancestors destroyed themselves and damn near destroyed us. Next thing you know, the liberals on Mars will be thinking in terms of interplanetary aid; and then in a century or two, and with tears of gratitude in their eyes, these bastard whites will programme a fleet of thermonuclear missiles for Mars. It has happened once. Only complete extermination can stop it happening again."

Rudlan Others looked at him. "History is only what we care to remember," he remarked obscurely. "And one man's beast may be another man's demigod."

"What do you mean by that? Are you trying to say that Vaney-ism is founded on a lie?"

"No. I'd be a fool if I were. I'm trying to tell you, Kord, that what we need—what we all need—is a sense of perspective. Perspective unclouded by dogma."

"I shall report this statement, and you will have the pleasure of transmitting my report."

"Do that." Rudlan Others indicated the attention light that was winking steadily on the telecommunications console. "Meanwhile, be a good fellow and don't sabotage *my* work. Keeping Mars informed is more immediately important than deciding the fate of homo sapiens on Terra."

"I'll be back!" snapped Kord Vengel furiously. "I'll be back with a hundred groups for priority transmission, personal and secret, to General Anders."

Rudlan Others sighed. "Go easy with the adjectives. Even generals, I'm sure, prefer hard facts."

CHAPTER SIXTEEN

Mirlena was relieved to find that the second communication session went much better. For one thing, practice was making it easier for her to use and understand the archaic language. Also, Kymri was helping—actively helping—to expand her vocabulary; while at the same time she was managing to regain a certain amount of psychological initiative. She had buried in the recesses of her mind that brief but unnerving evocation of the black slave/white master relationship. Now she was the efficient Dr. Stroza once more, intent not only upon exploring the mental attitudes and characteristics of the primitive white man but also upon demonstrating the vast literal and metaphorical gulf that lay between the expanding technological culture of Mars and the regressive fragments of civilization on Earth.

But there still remained a formidable barrier to understanding that Mirlena could do nothing about. Kymri was a prisoner in a cage. As such, he was suspicious of almost everything and resigned to his own destruction. Mirlena had appealed to both Kord Vengel and Streven Luse for Kymri to have a limited amount of freedom, if only for short periods. But, for different reasons, both men were agreed that Kymri should remain behind bars—the Political Officer because he regarded Kymri as a dangerous animal and the Chief Officer because his primary consideration was the safety of his vessel. He shuddered to think what might happen if, by some mischance, the savage managed to press a few buttons on the navigation deck or in the engine room.

So Mirlena had to make the best of trying to establish some element of friendship with a man behind bars—a man who was convinced that in the end his captors would simply kill him.

But a kind of friendship could and did develop because of one thing that Mirlena and Kymri had in common—an immense curiosity. Each was hungry for knowledge. Each became willing to trade knowledge for knowledge.

In the second communication session, Mirlena tried to explain to Kymri that he was in a space vessel in low orbit round the planet that was his home. Surprisingly, Kymri did not find this too difficult a notion to accept. But, of course, he demanded proof; and though proof was exasperatingly easy to provide, he could not be let out of his cage and taken to the nearest observation panel.

However, there was the fact of low G. Kymri had more or less adjusted to the weak field of synthetic gravitation. He knew that a similar condition existed nowhere on the world with which he was familiar. Therefore, he was inclined at least to seriously consider the explanation that was given to him—particularly when Mirlena, armed with perma pad and point, drew sketches of the space ship in orbit, of the planetary surface and of the probe that he had encountered in the forest.

She also brought him many photographs. Kymri had never seen photographs before and was impressed by the miraculous quality of the pictures. There were shots of the forest, which he recognized. There were shots of the sloop at touch-down and of the landing party carrying out the investigations. There were even shots of Kymri himself, being taken to the sloop shortly before the small exploratory vessel returned to orbit.

Surprisingly—at least, to Mirlena—he was well able to grasp the concept of space. He seemed already to be able to appreciate the fact that there was a multiplicity of worlds and that these black strangers in their great vessel had journeyed from a planet far away in the depths of eternal night. Oddly he found it difficult to understand how Earth and Mars could share the same sun, preferring his own private conviction that the visitors were not omniscient, that Mirlena was mistaken, and that Mars had a sun of its own.

Repeatedly, he had asked her to allow him outside the cage. Repeatedly, Mirlena had to refuse. But on an odd impulse, and in order to demonstrate her growing trust, Mirlena eventually broke the rule that no one should enter the cage unaccompanied.

Kymri was sitting despondently on the floor with his back to her. All the talking and all the strange ideas had made his head buzz; and once more he was depressed by the conviction that he would never leave this tiny prison alive.

Mirlena spoke to him twice, but he did not answer. Suddenly she felt a tremendous wave of sympathy for this strange creature who had borne so much with such fortitude. There were two locks on the cage, one electronically controlled, one manually controlled. The same key fitted both.

She looked at it wonderingly, hardly knowing how it came to be in her hand. Then with quick movements, she unlocked the door. She stepped into the cage, but Kymri appeared to pay no attention. Until she laid a hand on his shoulder.

Then he moved with incredible speed—and with incredible skill in a field of synthetic gravity. One moment he was sitting dejectedly on the floor. The next moment, using only one arm, he had pinioned both Mirlena's arms behind her back and his free hand was pressing lightly with the thumb on her throat and the fingers behind her ear.

"It is so easy to kill," he said softly. "So easy. The door is open, and some of your comrades would regret that Kymri op Kymriso enjoyed a brief freedom."

Mirlena was too shaken to say anything. One moment he was a despairing human being; but in the next he had become an efficient and dangerous machine. She felt the strength in his muscles. Earth strength. Far more powerful than any muscles that could be developed under the comparatively low gravity of Mars.

Earth strength! His vitality, his intensity, terrified her. She thought she was about to die, and was paralysed by sheer anticipation. There was a curious, warm lethargy in her limbs. Almost a desire to die. Which was the most frightening of all.

"It is easy to kill," Kymri went on. "But it is not the answer. I do not know why. Perhaps Godfred amuses himself." Suddenly, he released her, and was smiling. "Woman, you must not become weaker than you are—otherwise you will not live to a great ripeness. Secure the animal in its cage once more, and remove temptation from us both."

He watched, still smiling, as she retreated from the cage and locked the door behind her. Then she let out a sigh of relief, and noticed that her limbs were shaking.

"I do not understand," she said. "I do not understand why you did not escape when you had the opportunity."

He shrugged. "Where is there to go? Am I not trapped in a metal monster in the sky?"

CHAPTER SEVENTEEN

Streven Luse had called a meeting on the navigation deck. He could have used the saloon, which was also spacious; but the navigation deck had seemed more appropriate. Besides it was pleasant—and, perhaps, a welcome reminder of the significance of the expedition—to be able to be almost surrounded by transparent panels, on the other side of which lay great immensities of space shot through with the calm brilliance of an infinity of stars.

Present at the meeting were Mirlena Stroza, Meiron Menders, Tam Mbela, and Kord Vengel. It might turn out to be a stormy meeting, thought Captain Luse. He hoped the sight of the stars would have some tranquillizing effect.

"Let us not waste any time," he began, "for time is the one thing we cannot afford to waste. I do not have to remind you that this expedition has cost, in aggregate, almost one tenth of the industrial and scientific resources of Mars for several years. It is our duty to provide as high a return as possible upon investment—even if that return consists less of immediate material benefits than of sheer knowledge or information. You are all aware that, in fact, there was no single motive for Mars devoting so much energy to mounting our expedition to Earth. There was, of course, the fact that since we are on the threshold of relatively long-range space exploration, we needed some experience of the stresses of voyage and the techniques of exploration." He smiled thinly. "From that point of view, Earth was a natural target, since Earth-Mars jumps were carried out satisfactorily two thousand years ago, and because we already knew in great detail from the old records that, scientifically speaking, Earth is one of the most interesting, rewarding and accessible planets in the solar system. We knew that we could probably breathe air — far richer, even, than we are accustomed to breathing at home — and we thought that, because of our genetic history, there would be little danger of serious biological hazards. We knew also that Earth possesses — or possessed — an abundance of mineral wealth, including various rare metals, of which we are in short supply. Further, we believed that, partly because of the racist wars of two thousand years ago, which brought about the destruction of Luna, and partly because of the disappearance of Earth's magnetic field, with the resulting bombardment of high velocity particles, mankind would be extinct upon this planet. Thus, there would be no one to obstruct our exploration or to interfere with subsequent mining operations if, ultimately, such developments are justified."

He paused and looked at his companions. He had a shrewd idea what each of them would be thinking and, childishly, he was enjoying keeping them in suspense.

"Theoretically," he continued, "we should spend as much time as possible on paramagnetometric and seismic surveys. Then we should touch down at favourable locations for intensive investigation. And finally we should report on the condition of the remains of such major cities as escaped total destruction when the main fragments of Luna passed or fell. Also, in theory, we have a ninety-day limit in which to carry out all of these tasks." He smiled again. "Though we are all aware that ninety years — even ninety Martian years — would hardly be sufficient to do what needs to be done . . . Gentlemen—and Dr. Stroza—we are in the position of children who have managed to find their way into a sweets' factory. Surrounded as it were by wealth, and with little enough time at our disposal—no matter how we stretch it—we can only carry away what we can hastily cram into our pockets."

He paused again. "However, the position becomes more interesting and, paradoxically, more frustrating because we have discovered that the planet Earth is not dead. That it was not dead in the biological sense was apparent even before we locked into our first orbit. There are green patches in the relatively unscarred land mass of ancient Eurasia and in parts of South America. There are oceans, greatly reduced, but still oceans—a novel phenomenon to fortieth generation Martians—in which life may be presumed to exist . . .

"And, finally, there is this vast polar continent, mist-shrouded and tropical, which was once known as Antarctica. It is difficult for us to make a useful survey from altitude because of the density of the cloud formations and also because of the density of the forest that lies beneath them. Once this was a frozen continent. Before that, far back in geological time, it was a primitive rain forest. The pendulum of history swings and it is a rain forest once more.

"There are two important factors relating to Antarctica. The first is that, during all the long ascendancy of the white races, Antarctica was covered by ice and was virtually inaccessible. Its natural resources are—or were—unplundered. Of all the areas of Earth it is the one that is most attractive for a number of reasons. But, gentlemen and Dr. Stroza, as you are aware, there is a complication. Antarctica, uninhabited by man throughout the history of this planet, has now become a last refuge—now that the remainder of the planet is virtually uninhabitable—for what is left of terrestrial mankind. This is a sad and ironic situation. For us, as members of the first expedition from Mars to Earth, it is also an exciting and dangerous situation. Are we to leave Antarctica alone? Are we to investigate according to our original plan? Are we to seek out these people of Earth and learn what we can of their civilization—if, indeed, it can be called that. Or are we to avoid them and, if necessary, destroy those we accidentally meet? These are grave questions, yet we can afford little time to deliberate on them. I have spoken too long already. Let us hear what Dr. Stroza has to say. And gentlemen," he glanced meaningfully at Kord Vengel, "let us endeavour to evaluate impartially. There can be no value in personal prejudice."

Streven Luse sat back in a contour pod and motioned to Mirlena. She stood up, glanced briefly at the backcloth of stars and then nervously at her companions.

"You all know how we discovered the terrestrial who was brought back to orbit for investigation. If I do not remind you that his first act on encountering us was one of attempted aggression, then someone else will do so—doubtless drawing unsound conclusions between present occurrences and the historically documented aggression of the white races—an aggression which, it seems, was primarily responsible for the establishment of our own civilization on Mars."

"Objection!" snapped Kord Vengel.

"Overruled," said Streven Luse imperturbably. "This is simply a pooling of ideas. You may contribute your own presently. Proceed, Dr. Stroza."

"The point I wish to make," said Mirlena, "is that Kymri op Kymriso reacted normally to an abnormal situation, as any of us would do. It is impossible to draw a general conclusion from a single act of desperation."

Kord Vengel interrupted again. "Who is Kymri op Kymriso?" he demanded unnecessarily.

Mirlena smiled. "You know very well, Kord. Would you prefer to call him my little white savage?"

"That is exactly what he is—a white savage." Kord Vengel looked at his companions. "That is what we must remember if Dr. Stroza attempts to demonstrate that he has redeeming virtues."

"I do not wish to demonstrate anything—merely to give you the broad results of my investigations so far. If, of course, I am allowed to do so."

"Officer Vengel," said Captain Luse sharply, "if you cannot contain yourself until the proper time, you really will have to leave this meeting and allow the rest of us to get on with our business—possibly taking decisions which your presence and the benefit of your wisdom might have modified."

Kord Vengel glowered silently, sitting upright in his contour pod, which was hard to do since it had been designed for physical relaxation and the even distribution of stresses.

"In the course of my investigation of the white savage," went on Mirlena with a touch of sarcasm in her voice, "I took the trouble to analyse his language patterns, with considerable help from Rudlan Others, who ran a computer programme which enabled me to produce a lexicon. I have had copies of this lexicon made, and anyone who is interested, or who doubts the conclusions I draw, will be able to talk directly with Kymri op Kymriso and arrive at his own conclusions. This Earth language, I may say, corresponds roughly to early period Martian—that is to say, it derives from the dead language once known as English.

"Although my investigations are by no means complete—in a sense, they have barely begun—several interesting facts are already apparent. The first and most important is that, within the limitations of his environment, Kymri is a mature, intelligent and resourceful person. He mistrusts us quite as much as we mistrust him—in fact, he believes that we will kill him when we are tired of him—and so it is rather difficult to extract much concrete information concerning his background, his status in society or even the physical size of the socio-economic unit to which he belongs.

"However, I think I have succeeded in establishing a minimal personal trust between us." Mirlena paused for a moment, smiling to herself as she recalled the occasion when, at Kymri's request, she had unzipped her shipboard suit and the even more disconcerting occasion when she had entered his cage. But these were personal items of experience—the kind that Kord Vengel could transform into dynamite—and she had no intention of revealing them to anyone at all. "A trust, at least, which enables us to talk peacefully and to barter a limited amount of information. I have explained to him that he is now in a space ship and that we are travellers from another world. He is able to comprehend space travel and does not have any difficulty in accepting the existence of other planets, though he appears to believe that different planets cannot share the same sun. He has some rudimentary awareness of the existence of science—particularly what he calls electrics—and can understand that it is possible to devise complex machines. He destroyed our probe in the belief that it was not a machine but a sky beast. At first, he thought the entire experience was what he defines as an elsdykik—that is to say, an illusion. I had some trouble finding a parallel for this word. Most likely, it is a corruption of L.S.D. kick. L.S.D. is short for lysergic acid diethylamide, a drug that is still occasionally used as an hallucinogen.

"When Kymri finally decided our probe was not the result of an elsdykik, he tried to destroy it because it seemed to correspond to the folklore descriptions of the nuclear missiles that were used to destroy terrestrial cities two thousand years ago. He was thus prepared to sacrifice his own life in defence of Noi Lantis—a corruption of New Atlantis—the city-state to which he belongs. Alternatively, he was half-inclined to believe that it was part of a joke being played upon him by the local deity—apparently a rather cruel being with a perverted sense of humour whose name is Godfred. I personally could find no equivalent for Godfred in early Martian or dead English. But, on the basis of other corrupted or compounded words, the computer has equated it with two words, God and Freud.

"It is several years since my college programme on the early history of psychiatry, but I recall that about a century before negro emancipation on Earth, there was a brilliant American negro psychiatrist called Sigma Freud. Because she was black and a woman, she experienced great difficulty practising in New York. Eventually, after considerable persecution, she fled to Vienna in the central European feudal state of Austria and sought political asylum. Witchcraft was very popular in Austria at that time; and Sigma Freud, having accidentally acquired a considerable reputation as a witch, was allowed to practice psychiatry unmolested. It was during this period that she published her most important works.

"I mention such matters at length because this important background material plus the known facts will enable us to build up a useful model of the kind of society to which Kymri op Kymriso belongs."

Mirlena looked at her companions, sensing their impatience. She had been playing for time, and they knew it. Probably, they also knew why. She was afraid, simply afraid, of the decision that might be taken. The extreme reaction would be supplied by Kord Vengel, who would advocate genocide or, at least, the destruction of any more white people or any white cities encountered. She did not believe it would ever come to that; but still it was a possibility. Streven Luse and Meiron Menders, she felt, would be more inclined to ignore the terrestrials and simply pursue the original investigation programme. If the terrestrials did not interfere, well and good. But if they did interfere, then they would be killed. Mirlena did not want that either, though it was certainly better than a policy of extermination. Perhaps Tam Mbela was a potential ally. As a biologist, he ought to have an interest in the preservation and investigation of *all* life found on the planet Earth.

Ideally, Mirlena wanted the expedition to devote as much time as possible to the investigation of Noi Lantis and its inhabitants. Here was a golden opportunity to find out what the enigmatic white race had really been like. Of course, their regressive descendants would not correspond in either attitudes or accomplishments to the people who had once maintained a planet-wide civilization. But at least it would be possible to trace back, and by patient assembly of evidence reconstruct something of the psychic profile of that aggressive race that had shown man the way to the stars.

Mirlena looked at her companions and realized that she would only harm her own case by further delays. She took a deep breath and prepared to deliver the summary of her findings.

"Having filled in a little of the background, I will now go

straight on to my general conclusions. If there is serious disagreement about them, I will give my justifications later.

"First. Kymri op Kymriso himself. So far as can be ascertained, and within the frame reference of his culture level, there are no serious psychic abnormalities. He appears to be an intelligent being with considerable race-loyalty. From what he has said or hinted—and since we are potential enemies he has not disclosed a great deal—it would seem that Noi Lantis is a small, self-sufficient unit ruled by monarchy and priesthood. The priests are the custodians of such elementary science as has been preserved. Simple machines are known and used, but the resources of Noi Lantis are not geared for technological development. Clearly Noi Lantis is in cultural decline and cannot, either now or in the future, develop any threat to the security of Mars. From a scientific point of view, I suggest we have a unique opportunity —which may well have disappeared by the time regular Martian traffic is established with Earth—for investigating the behaviour of a primitive white people and perhaps adding significantly to our knowledge of terrestrial history."

"Thank you Dr. Stroza," said Captain Luse drily. "As I remarked earlier, time is one thing we cannot afford to waste. Neither," and he looked at Kord Vengel, "can we afford to quarrel among ourselves. Whatever programme is decided upon, we must all commit ourselves to it wholeheartedly . . . Meiron, as physicist, kindly give us your views."

Meiron Menders, at twenty-six Martian years old, was the youngest man present. Though a dedicated and brilliant physicist, he had a remarkable variety of other interests. In thinking that he would be antipathetic to her project, Mirlena had underestimated him.

"I have deliberately avoided contact with Kymri," said Meiron, "because I felt that he might easily be confused by too many people. So the only data available to me is what Dr. Stroza has supplied. As a physicist, I have enough priority work to occupy me for some considerable time, so there is no need of diversions. For example, I would like to make detailed investigation of the effects of the impact of Lunar fragments in the equatorial regions, where the greatest damage was done. I would also like to make intensive seismic surveys of selected areas. I would also like to acquire large samples of titanium, aluminium and other metals or ores that are virtually unobtainable on Mars. In short, and like everyone else, I have too much work and too little time in which to do it.

"So why should I concern myself about primitive white people who are unlikely to be able to contribute to my scientific knowledge?" He paused, and looked solemnly at Mirlena, who was trying to conceal her disappointment. Then he continued: "I will tell you why. Because I think the discovery of this simple white man is potentially more important than any scientific revelations this planet has to offer. Dr. Stroza says that his culture is in a long decline. This may be so, or it may not be so. But for the sake of everyone on Mars it is our duty to find out. Individual life is short, but racial existence is long. It may be that in the far future, black Martians and white Terrans will have to try to learn to live with each other yet again."

"Admirably put," observed Captain Luse. He turned to Tam Mbela, the white-haired biologist. "Well, Tam, what about you?"

Tam Mbela grinned. "I'm afraid I have a vested interest. The tropical forests down there are a biologist's paradise. I could find enough work to last me ten years without venturing more than a kilometre from the touch-down point . . . Mind you, I am not too keen on trying to fraternize with savages. What if they play rough, as this one tried to do? It is easy enough to deal with one savage. But could we deal with a hundred or two hundred? We have the weapons, but they know the forest. I am not in favour of attempting to establish contact because I think it could jeopardize the entire expedition."

"A good point. A very good point," said the Captain. "It has probably occurred to everyone, but I'm glad you brought it up . . . Now, Kord," he smiled, "I see you have been extraordinarily patient, and it is time you had your say."

Oddly, at this stage, Kord Vengel seemed quite relaxed. When he spoke, it was softly and persuasively, with an air of a man who is concerned only with facts and rational solutions to problems.

"Unlike Dr. Stroza, I think I can state my case briefly. First, I agree with Meiron Menders that, whatever else we do, we cannot afford to ignore these primitive whites. You all know my basic attitude. This degenerate and paranoid race—forgive me if I borrow some of your jargon, Dr. Stroza—has threatened us with extinction before; and I have no doubt that, given half a chance, it would do so again. That is why we must find out the strength and the potential of these people who managed to survive a holocaust of their own making. If, as I suspect, these regressive descendants are as destructive as their ancestors, there can hardly be any choice for us. We shall have to exterminate them. It is foreseeable that there will be other expeditions from Mars; and if, as seems possible, Earth still has some material wealth to offer, we Martians may ultimately establish an industrial colony, perhaps here in Antarctica.

"Therefore the matter must be settled now. We cannot jeopardize the future. I know that many people on this vessel regard me as a fanatic. Well, perhaps I am fanatical. I believe in the principles of Vaneyism and I believe in maintaining the purity of our race. Two thousand years ago, we survived by the skin of our teeth and by the sheer selfless courage of those first black Martian colonists. They needed material help from Earth. Instead they received interplanetary missiles. They needed brotherhood, and they received enmity. That is history. We should do well to remember it.

"Finally, there is for me personally the most telling fact of all." He paused, then went on impressively. "Gentlemen, Dr. Stroza, there is something in the blood that cannot be expressed in words. Since encountering this savage, I have begun to think of myself as not just a man but a black man. It is a sad thing. The natural enmity between the white and black races doubtless goes back to the dawn of history. There is nothing we can do about it. I sense that it is as strong in the savage as it is in me. Whatever else we do, we cannot allow this ancient hostility to threaten our existence yet again. Savages are no threat. But

84

civilized savages—aided, perhaps, by misguided do-gooders—could in the future easily release a new cycle of destruction. That is all I have to say."

"And you seem to have said it very well," remarked Streven Luse with a note of surprise in his voice. He looked at each of his companions intently. "As the person directly responsible for the success or failure of this expedition, it is my duty, having heard your advice and observations, to decide our future course of action. I agree that we cannot ignore these people of Noi Lantis. I agree that we cannot hazard the expedition by committing our resources too heavily in an effort to establish contact and investigate the strength of their society. Altogether, we have sixteen people aboard this vessel. I propose to commit not more than four to the task of finding out the numbers and general level of development of these white people. Further, I am prepared to allow fifteen days for the survey, which will start as soon as possible. I am reluctant to hazard even four lives and I refuse to risk more. Dr. Stroza, as our psychologist, has considerable knowledge of anthropology and other relevant studies. She is an essential member of the investigation team. Kord Vengel, as Political Officer, will be able to assess the political and racial implications. The remaining two members will, I hope, be selected from suitable volunteers. I don't think I need to say anything more for the present."

Mirlena was both elated and depressed. She had won another battle but, noting the gleam of triumph in Kord Vengel's eyes, she was afraid that she still might be losing the war. The fact that further investigation had now been decided upon was wonderful; but the fact that Kord Vengel was to be an essential member of the team was disastrous. She could not forgive Streven Luse for that; though she realized, when she thought about it calmly, that Marsbase had probably demanded Kord's inclusion.

She knew that he would be entering into the white man's world with his mind already made up. Prejudice, hatred and Vaneyism were a powerful combination. Doubtless Kord would already be

85

composing a report recommending extermination even before he set foot in Noi Lantis.

Still, a lot could happen in fifteen days. Perhaps, even, a lot could happen to Kord Vengel.

CHAPTER EIGHTEEN

Kymri gazed at the emerald forest, rejoicing in its beauty, not entirely sure if he were alive or dead. He gave silent thanks to Godfred for favours received. Basically, it did not matter whether he was alive or dead. All that mattered was that the illusion—if it was an illusion—wore such a wonderfully convincing aspect of reality.

His cloak of firebird feathers had been restored to him, along with the leather triangles of manhood. It hardly mattered that he lacked a spear and that his ankles had been roped to each other so that he could not run. It was enough to feel the fine rain on his face, to sniff the scents of the forest and to listen to all the secret whisperings of life and growth.

Again, the sloop had touched down very near to the dead probe. Besides Kymri, the sloop had brought Mirlena, Kord Vengel, Rudlan Others and Garl Sinjorge, an assistant physicist. Rudlan and Garl had been chosen from seven volunteers. They had been chosen because Streven Luse considered them to be relatively expendable.

The journey from orbit down to earth had held much terror for Kymri. Again he had been compelled to wear a space suit which, in itself, seemed to him to be a particularly excruciating form of torture. But now he was back in his own element. The ordeal had been worth it.

Under normal gravity, his limbs felt like the limbs of a man once more. He sprang joyfully into the air, luxuriating in the speed and force with which his feet hit the ground. The Martians, each feeling as if they carried invisible and heavy burdens upon their backs, regarded him enviously. Though they had undergone extensive training to help them withstand Earth gravity, the strain of remaining upright and walking fairly slowly was about as much as they could bear.

Kymri had struck a bargain with Mirlena. She had told him that four Martians, including herself, were to be sent to Noi Lantis to learn about its people and their customs; and he had reasoned that, despite their powerful weapons and their knowledge of machines, four Martians could not constitute a serious threat to a city of more than twelve thousand people.

Of course, it might be a trap; and the rest of the Martians might follow secretly—no one had told him how many there were in the entire expedition—but even so, the people of Noi Lantis had a formidable ally in the forest itself. For it was obvious that these black-skinned creatures were not forest people. So, if trouble should start, Godfred would doubtless suggest some interesting ways of dealing with it.

Besides, if he had not agreed to take these strangers to Noi Lantis, they could easily have killed him and still, perhaps, have found their own way to the city—probably by sending a sky monster to look for it. Better to escort the Martians himself, save his own life and, if need be, warn and advise his people.

Part of the deal made between Kymri and Mirlena was that he should have the freedom to look around the space ship in which he had been kept prisoner. This was strenuously opposed both by Streven Luse and Kord Vengel. But Kymri, realizing vaguely that for once he was in a position to insist, remained firm. No freedom on the space ship, no guide to Noi Lantis. Eventually

Mirlena persuaded Captain Luse to allow Kymri the freedom of the ship, provided that he was accompanied at all times by two armed Martians.

Closed circuit television, intercom, electrics, manual telescopes, infra-red cookers, refrigeration—all these marvels made his head ache. But, most breath-taking of all, were the views through the observation panels. First, the glowing ball that was Earth rolling smoothly below, huge and silent and perfectly formed, unreal and hypnotic, and at times like an all-seeing eye. Kymri watched several sunrises, each seeming to be more beautiful than the last. Then he went to the darkside panels and gazed and gazed at the overwhelming intensity of the stars.

On Earth he rarely saw stars, for the sky was nearly always cloudy; and the occasional patches of relatively clear sky revealed nothing compared to what he could see free from the limitations of atmosphere. The stars were beautiful—too beautiful. Tears rolled down his face, to the amazement of his guards, but he was not even aware that he was crying. He was drunk with wonder, excited beyond endurance by an odd tranquillity. It was the greatest thing that had ever happened to him in his life. One day, he vowed, he would see the stars from such a platform again. One day, he, too, would learn the secrets of vessels that could sail out across the oceans of the night.

To everyone's surprise—except Mirlena—Kymri gave no trouble during his few hours of freedom. It was a great disappointment to Kord Vengel. His finger had been itching to hit the button of his needle gun.

Kymri's private bargain with Mirlena had been a complex one. He had agreed to lead the investigation team to Noi Lantis and to do all within his power to ensure the safety of the Martians and to create friendly relations between them and the occupants of the city. Mirlena, for her part, had promised to supply as much information about electrics, medicine and basic chemistry as the Noi Lantians could use or require.

It was just as well that Streven Luse did not know of the arrangement. If he had suspected that Mirlena would agree to give the white savages information that might enable them to industrialize within a generation, he might have been more sympathetic to Kord Vengel's original extermination plans.

Now, as Kymri felt the warm wet earth beneath his feet and watched the awkward movements of the Martians, he began to feel relaxed for the first time in many days. If the black woman kept faith, there would be great happenings in Noi Lantis in the coming years. If she did not keep faith, then at least four Martians would not return to their home across the sky.

CHAPTER NINETEEN

"Now, little one," said Kord Vengel to Kymri, "let us have a demonstration so that we may understand each other perfectly."

Apart from Mirlena, Kord Vengel was the only other Martian who had taken the trouble to learn to speak to Kymri in his own language. With some instruction and the aid of Mirlena's lexicon, he had given himself a crash course which had involved losing many hours of sleep. He had achieved proficiency in a remarkably short time, and felt that the effort was worth it. He did not want Mirlena and Kymri saying things to each other that he could not understand.

The party had reached the probe whose cameras Kymri had destroyed before the sloop's first touch-down. Already the forest was claiming it. Green tendrils wound round the three mighty legs on which it stood. Bird droppings were in evidence on the surface of the great black sphere.

Kymri's primitive sense of direction required that he should start the return journey to Noi Lantis from the place where the sky-beast had landed, since it was that part of the forest in which he had been captured. There were no tracks to follow—even if one made a track, the forest could obliterate it in a single after-noon—nor was it easy to navigate by the position of the sun, since the sun was rarely visible. All that remained was a kind of unconscious record of the outward journey, measured perhaps in footsteps, time, the rise and fall of the land, or a combination of all three. Kymri did not know how his 'homing' instinct oper-ated. He only knew that he possessed it and that it rarely failed.

But before the trek to Noi Lantis began—and at the rate the Martians could travel it would probably take three days—Kord Vengel was intent upon impressing Kymri with a demonstration of power, in case the little white savage had any ideas of treachery.

The Political Officer carried a sweep rifle, a weapon which operated on the laser principle and which could bring a devastat-ingly high concentration of radiant energy to bear on any target up to a distance of about five hundred metres.

"It may have occurred to you to play tricks upon us," said Kord Vengel. "In which case you should be aware of the kind of weapons with which we can retaliate. For example, if you are tempted to lead us into an ambush, you should know that this thing I carry can blind or maim more than a hundred men in less time than it takes one of you people to hurl a spear."

Kymri was not looking at Kord Vengel. His eyes seemed to be focussed on the green roof of the forest, high above the Political Officer's head—almost as if he disdained even to consider the warning that was given to him.

Kord was irritated. It seemed to him that the white savage was taking his natural insolence just a little too far.

He selected a tree, aimed the sweep rifle at its base a little above ground level and pressed the discharge stud. The tree flamed briefly, then its trunk came crashing into the temporary clearing created by the probe's touch down.

Still Kymri did not appear to be greatly impressed. Still his attention was fixed high above Kord Vengel's head.

Mirlena said in a somewhat high voice: "That is quite enough, Kord. I think Kymri is already aware that we have a great deal of power at our disposal."

Kord Vengel ignored her. His eyes were on Kymri. "Well, joker," he said softly, "let us see how strong your nerves are."

He aimed the sweep rifle rapidly and pressed the stud twice. A fountain of fire leaped up from the ground not more than a métre from Kymri's left foot. Then there was another gout of flame near his right foot.

Kymri started and jumped forward with an anxious expression on his face. The Political Officer laughed and half turned to his companions as if inviting them to share his amusement at the discomfiture of the white savage.

In that moment, there was a rustle somewhere and a blur of movement. Kymri launched himself like a missile through the air at Kord Vengel. His head hit the unprepared Political Officer in the chest. Kord Vengel uttered an agonized grunt, and both men fell sprawling to the ground, Kord already grappling fiercely, but hindered by the terrible G force that was part of Kymri's normal environment.

The tree springer barely missed them. Its armoured tail delivered an excruciating blow to Kymri's shoulder.

Fortunately, Garl Sinjorge had fast reactions. He, too, carried a sweep rifle. With it, he almost severed the head of the monstrous tree springer from its body. The stench of burning flesh and the thrashing of the already dead body in such close proximity instantly diverted Kord Vengel from his attempt to kill Kymri. He scrambled to his feet, horrified, and backed cautiously away.

Kymri also picked himself up, and regarded the tree springer calmly. Kord Vengel's sweep rifle lay under the now twitching and incredibly massive body of the beast. Kymri stepped forward and with some difficulty pulled the sweep rifle clear. Its barrel was twisted slightly and, though Kymri did not know it, it was now no more than useless scrap. Without expression or comment, he handed the weapon to Kord.

Garl shuddered. "Where did that disgusting creature come from?" He looked up.

Mirlena was watching Kymri. "You knew it was going to fall, didn't you?"

"Yes."

"Why did you not warn us?"

"You would have moved. A tree springer that falls and misses may become a dead tree springer. It is too slow for combat on the ground. But a tree springer that stays aloft may fall later, when none are aware of its presence . . . I could have killed the creature with a blow of my foot if your man had not held me."

Mirlena said: "You were trying to save his life?"

Kymri laughed. "Surely all here are witnesses. I *did* save the man's life. Thus one observes Godfred's fine sense of humour in requiring me to do so."

Kord Vengel was shaking. He was shaking for two reasons. The first was that he had been in physical contact with a white man for the first time in his life, and the second was that he had been close to death.

"Savage," he said evenly, "I will remember your action. If you had warned me, I could have slain the beast with my weapon. Perhaps it amused you to risk both our lives in this way."

"Did it not also amuse you to test me with the machine that makes blue fire?" enquired Kymri with a thin smile. "But a man with a terrible weapon is still no more than a man, Kord Vengel. It is something to remember."

"He is right, Kord," said Mirlena gently. "Let us all try to trust each other. It is necessary for our survival."

He looked at her coldly. "Would you trust me, Mirlena?"

"I know that you are a brave man. On this strange world, which has dangers we Martians cannot conceive or anticipate, I am very glad of your company."

Rudlan Others and Garl Sinjorge had been inspecting the dead beast. There was no wild creature so large or so fearsome on Mars. Indeed Mars possessed very few indigenous wild animals. Originally, some domestic animals and a few small wild things such as rabbits and pheasants and even a special breed of reindeer had been imported from Earth. These kind of creatures could survive in cold, thin-air conditions upon sparse and simple vegetation. But until the climatic engineering programme was completed—and altogether it took nearly two centuries—Mars was as unhospitable as the tropical rain forest of Antarctica was fertile. The Martians had had to pit themselves against the elements but not against creatures of prey. They would have to do a lot of re-thinking if they were to survive on Earth.

The tree springer was one of the most ugly and dangerous beasts of the forest. Ironically, it was a descendant of that extinct but once harmless and inoffensive creature, the armadillo.

The series of catastrophes that had begun on Earth two thousand years ago—beginning with the War of the Black Rising, which resulted in the destruction of Luna and the partial devastation of the Earth—had produced many terrible and strange consequences. The patterns and balance of land masses and oceans were changed drastically. Temperate zones became sun-baked deserts. The Pacific Ocean, bombarded with stray chunks of Luna, produced tidal waves that battered the very heights of the Andes, swallowed islands, engulfed Japan, swamped China and Australia, destroyed New Zealand and Indonesia, created vast clusters of volcanoes, generated earthquakes beyond anything experienced in the history of man, and threw billions of tons of dust and boiling water up into the thin reaches of the atmosphere. Lowlands were submerged, new land masses rose convulsively in the Atlantic, the Mediterranean drained, and—paradoxically—Antarctica began to melt. Seven thousand million human beings perished in less than six months, the majority of the remainder merely took longer to die. Some found high ground and finally baked, some found low ground and finally starved. But life is tenacious. Antarctica grew a green umbrella to cover and sustain all who might reach its sanctuary.

As if man's inhumanity to man were not enough, Nature herself accelerated the devastation, the trauma, the change. Earth's magnetic field had been constantly weakening and was no longer able to trap the high energy particles streaming out from the sun. As the magnetic lines of force became weaker, the Van Allen radiation belt began to dissipate, and Earth was subjected to increasing bombardment from that vast cosmic nuclear reactor that had hitherto sustained life and maintained relative organic stability.

Mutation followed upon devastation. Rats with two heads, or no eyes, or three legs or whiplike, prehensile tails nibbled away at what was left of civilization. Whales died because of radio-active plankton. Elephants were annihilated by ants. Lions fled howling from herds of hungry and omnivorous antelope. The entire animal kingdom was in bizarre ferment.

And the armadillo, timid and shy, eater of insects, worms, roots, responded with amazing speed to the dreadful stimulus of comparative torrents of radiation. Its armour thickened, it grew huge and carnivorous. It discovered that, though it lacked speed, its terrible bulk could be used to kill any prey, demolish any enemy. It learned to climb stout trees and wait patiently until something passed below. Then it would spring or drop and gorge itself upon the pulped remains. Until next time.

Mirlena stood with the rest, gazing with awe at the dreadful remains of the tree springer.

"Are there many such beasts in the forest?" she asked Kymri.

"Many," he answered cheerfully. "But a man learns to sense their presence, or lives but briefly. Besides, there is the stink of decay. Also, they cannot easily fit their shapes to the shape of a tree . . . Tree springers are bad, but the dragons are worse, and the worst of all are winged spiders. A man may cheat the tree springer, avoid the charge of the dragon; but with the winged spider, his only hope is to remain motionless and contemplate the humour of Godfred."

"How many kilometres—I'm sorry—how many kaymets is it to Noi Lantis?"

"Enough," said Kymri. "Perhaps thirty. One hard day's journey for me. Perhaps three days' journey for you and your companions. Perhaps more. But first there is work to be done."

Mirlena was surprised. "What kind of work?"

"Am I not unarmed, and are you not my guests? I must make weapons—a spear, at least—for your protection."

CHAPTER TWENTY

The walled city of Noi Lantis, with its cascade of stone towers and glass-panelled domes, seemed at a distance like a crust of multi-coloured jewels against the perennial green of the forest. The Martians, astounded, stood and gazed at it across stretches of cleared land outside the city walls where crops grew and various types of small cattle grazed under the watchful eyes of armed herdsmen.

The journey through the forest had taken longer even than Kymri had predicted. Although the Martians had trained rigorously to enable them to withstand Earth gravity, their training had not fitted them for the terrible endurance of travelling by foot for long periods at a time through country that, to them, seemed dizzily explosive with a bewildering variety of life-forms.

On the Martian plains it was possible to travel many kilometres without seeing any living thing apart from mosses, short grass and patches of heather. To see half a dozen rabbits was unusual. To see reindeer was memorable.

But here on Earth it seemed that a multitude of wild things, some large, some small, some harmless, some dangerous, were to be encountered with every few footsteps. As they passed noisily through the forest, Kymri had remarked on the scarcity of birds and animals, blaming the noise of their progress for driving the wild creatures away. But the Martians were dazed by the sheer fertility of this mist-shrouded patch of a planet that they had formerly supposed to be dead. They saw more animals in the course of a single afternoon than they had seen in the rest of their lives.

Apart from the episode of the tree springer, the first day's march passed without any dramatic incident. Kymri caught a harmless purple ring snake and presented it to Mirlena, showing her how to wind it round her arm like a bracelet, where it would rest quietly until it became hungry for more flies. Although she was wearing a semi-armoured trek suit which protected her from neck to ankles, she seemed to feel the clammy touch of the reptile even through the metal-reinforced fabric. After a time, she surreptitiously dumped the snake, and Kymri pretended not to notice.

Besides their weapons, the Martians carried lightweight tents, sleeping bags, food concentrates, a small radio transceiver, and some basic medical supplies. Distributed between four people as loads in carefully designed rucksacks, these possessions were very light. Nevertheless, they were heavy enough to trouble the Martians. When Kymri became aware of their difficulties, he volunteered to carry all four rucksacks himself. He proposed to sling them on a wooden pole and balance the pole across one of his shoulders.

But neither Kord Vengel nor Garl Sinjorge were disposed to accept help from or acknowledge the physical superiority of a white savage of Earth. Mirlena and Rudlan Others were not so proud. Gratefully, they handed their rucksacks to Kymri and marvelled as he walked along with apparent unconcern, holding the straps of both rucksacks in one hand.

The rope that bound Kymri's ankles so that he could not run had been cut off at Mirlena's insistence and, surprisingly, with little protest from Kord Vengel. It kept catching on snags in the ground, causing Kymri to fall over and making the skin round his ankles sore. Even the Political Officer began to appreciate the absurdity of so handicapping a man upon whom their lives might suddenly depend.

With the approach of darkness the two tents were set up and the evening meal was taken. There now remained the delicate problem of sleeping arrangements and night watch. Garl Sinjorge had had the foresight to bring with him a length of perimeter alarm wire, complete with insulated pegs, bell, and high voltage cells. The alarm wire was pegged in a circle round the tents. If anything touched it during the night, it would simultaneously start the bell ringing and collect a jolt of electricity. But no one—and particularly Kymri, when the system was explained to him—felt that this would give adequate protection. Also, there did not appear to be a great deal of benefit to be obtained by the Martians taking turns to watch, since they were unfamiliar with the night sounds of the forest and with creatures of prey. They could hardly expect to be able to distinguish between what was harmless and what was dangerous.

In the end, it was decided that Kymri would sleep outside the tents with each Martian taking turns to sit by him for a spell, wide awake. Kymri was a light sleeper and, in any case, would probably recognize subconsciously any immediate danger, since he had been accustomed to spending nights in the forest by himself. Alternatively, if the Martian on duty saw or heard anything which seemed dangerous, he had only to rouse Kymri to have his suspicions confirmed or denied. From Kord Vengel's point of view, there was the added bonus that with one Martian permanently on watch, Kymri would not be able to slip away in the dark.

Rudlan Others took the first watch, Garl Sinjorge took the second, Kord Vengel took the third and Mirlena took the final pre-dawn watch. During the course of the night, there was an almost unending murmur of background noise and the occasional relatively distant sounds of small nocturnal struggles. On this, their first night in a terrestrial forest, the Martians were understandably apprehensive, and tended to waken Kymri whenever they heard the slightest rustle. But, after a time, each of the watchers gained a little more confidence—particularly when Kymri patiently and constantly affirmed that he was already aware of the noises for which they had roused him.

Shortly after Mirlena came to sit by him, there was a sudden movement and a slithering within the perimeter.

"Snake," whispered Kymri softly, and instantly alert. "Do not move."

Mirlena stifled a gasp. "I'm—I'm afraid." She managed to keep her voice to a whisper, but it took considerable effort. "Shouldn't we wake the others?"

"Why? They seal their little cloth houses. The snake cannot enter."

"I'm still very much afraid . . . Is it a dangerous snake?"

"I don't know. The snake does not know if we are dangerous also. Let us hope it has eaten."

Kymri's hand found Mirlena's in the darkness and held it reassuringly. She was trembling. He smiled to himself. "All skin is black in the night," he whispered. "So, briefly, we are of one race . . . Do not be afraid too much, sweet one, I will destroy that which tries to harm you. Stay still, that is all."

Kymri felt a sudden, heavy, rippling movement over his legs. He could see nothing at all in the blackness. Nor could the snake. From the weight and the thickness of its body, it seemed to be a big one.

Mirlena's hand tightened in his spasmodically as the snake began to pass over her trek suit. It was not only a very thick reptile, it was a very long one. In the darkness it seemed long enough to encircle the forest. Centuries passed while it slithered across the legs of the white savage and the black Martian woman. Presently, it slithered away under the perimeter wire without setting off the alarm or collecting a jolt.

Miraculously, Mirlena managed to contain her shaking until the creature had gone. Then she fell, quivering and sobbing silently into Kymri's arms.

"Sweet one," he soothed, "sweet one, there is no danger now. The thing has gone. We do not interest it."

"It seemed endless. Was it—was it a dangerous creature?"

"Condasnake, I think. It likes water. When it is hungry, it can crush anything that lives . . . Very big condasnake. I have not seen many."

Even through the thick trek suit, Kymri was disturbingly aware of the living, quivering body of the woman. When he had first encountered Mirlena, he had thought her terrifying. Later, he had decided that she was merely ugly. The thick lips, the broad nostrils, the prominent cheek bones—none of these conformed to the accepted standards of beauty that prevailed in Noi Lantis.

But, in the darkness of the night and with enmity temporarily abolished by the bond of shared danger, he knew that Mirlena was beautiful.

He held her firmly until the sobbing and the shaking had subsided. Then he stroked her hair—the short, stiff and oddly fragrant growth that curled magically like black moss over her head—and kissed her ear, and felt the now lovely cheek bones and the exciting curve of the nostrils.

She did not draw away.

"Kymri," she whispered, "you must not—"

"Say nothing. There is nothing to say."

His hand touched the breast beneath the trek suit. Not even the thick fabric could imprison its life, the sheer leap of its response.

Despite the disoriented computer that still tried to function in her head, Mirlena's hand achieved independence of decision and action. It slid to the zip-lock of the trek suit, and pulled it down from neck to groin.

Breasts shivered and danced beneath the power and gentleness of insistently exploring hands.

The strength ebbed from Mirlena's limbs. Her body became liquid and heavy. Heavier even than with Earth gravity. Heavy with all the weight of a million years, the ancient music of the blood. She moaned softly. The computer stopped computing, and rational thought was annihilated.

There was a great sweetness in her body, a greater sweetness in her lips and the serpent tongue that reared with impudence and challenge and hunger from its lair. But there was the greatest sweetness of all between her legs.

In thrall, Kymri explored it, rejoicing that the urgent hardness of his flesh should find a matching urgency that, in the blackness of the night, made both man and woman coalesce through the blacker ecstasy of passion.

When it was over, they lay together silently, flesh within flesh, waiting for the agonizing sweetness to drain from their bodies, waiting for reason to return. When it was over, they were each appalled by a moment of history.

Mirlena thought vaguely of two thousand years of tabu. Lying under a white man's body, touching him tenderly with knees, thighs, belly, lips, she thought of two thousand years of tabu and of all the tabu and tragedy before then, lost in time and the death of a civilization.

Tears were in her eyes. She stirred. Sensing a sudden withdrawal, Kymri himself withdrew. The contact was broken. The spell was over. Mirlena drew up her zip-lock.

"Say nothing," whispered Kymri again. "Say nothing. But remember, as I will remember."

Already, the darkness of the forest was turning into greyness. Already, the half light was penetrating the great green roof. Presently, the chattering of the birds increased as the greyness paled.

Presently, the black Martian and the white Terran looked at each other . . .

And were ashamed . . .

. . .

Despite the noises and activities of the night, when they had completed their watches, the Martians had managed to get some rest and snatches of sleep in their sealed tents. They had not been aware of the intrusion of the condasnake, nor—judging from their reactions— had they been aware of any exchange between Kymri and Mirlena.

All such sounds—and, Mirlena recollected apprehensively, there were many—must have been lost against the general background of forest noises. Which was indeed fortunate. For she had no illusions about what Kord Vengel's reactions would be. Since his philosophy could not accept the notion of mutual attraction between white and black, he would have cried rape—regardless of what Mirlena might have said. And then there would have been the late irony of negroes lynching a white man.

But the night held its secrets well, and no one was aware either of the closeness of death or the closeness of love.

After a quick breakfast, the Martians exercised limbs that were still aching from the effects of Earth gravity, then they packed their gear and were ready to march. For a time, Kymri and Mirlena avoided looking at each other. But when, eventually, they did exchange glances, each was relieved to find that the other was still an alien.

Perhaps, thought Mirlena, it was as Kymri had said. Only in the darkness could they be of one race.

Before the second day's trek began, they received a call from the main space ship, still in orbit. Besides checking that all was well with the ground party, Streven Luse advised them that he was recalling the sloop to orbit by remote control. He proposed to use it to put down another exploration party when his orbit was favourable for a down trajectory to the North American continent. He hoped to find a suitable touch-down area near what was once New York. It was high time that an investigation was made of the remains of a major city.

Rudlan Others reported back that all was well with the Noi Lantis expedition thus far. He did not mention the encounter with the tree springer, but contented himself with saying that progress was good and that Kymri was co-operating. Captain Luse again reminded the party that they were operating under a strict time limit and said that he would do his best to make radio contact once a day. If, for any reason, there was a breakdown in radio communication, the sloop would rendezvous as close as possible to its original touch-down shortly after dawn on the sixteenth day. He also said that if, in the opinion of the ground party, it was safe to rendezvous closer to Noi Lantis, he would need to know at least three days before touch-down, and the ground transceiver would have to be used as a continuous radio beacon.

With the conclusion of radio contact, the second day's journey began. More ground was covered than on the first day, partly because the Martians were beginning to adjust their muscles better and partly because the terrain itself was a little easier. There were no serious encounters with wild animals; but Kord Vengel, now acutely conscious of the existence of tree springers, had the satisfaction of dropping two with his needle pistol. They did not represent any threat to the party, since no one had to pass directly underneath. But Kord destroyed them for personal reasons. He had taken an abnormal dislike to the creatures not only because one of them had tried to kill him but because it had made him look foolish in the eyes of the savage.

The sleeping and watch arrangements for the second night were as for the first. Again the perimeter wire was set up. Again Kymri slept outside the tents, and again Mirlena took the pre-dawn watch.

But Kymri did not attempt to touch her. They sat side by side in the darkness, mostly silent, but occasionally talking quietly. Neither of them referred to the events of the previous night. Instead, Mirlena spoke a little of life on Mars and tried to give some impression of the extent and complexity of Martian cities. She even told him about the old bubble cities in the early days of colonization before the climatic engineering programme had provided enough oxygen-rich air and enough warmth for Martians to be able to venture freely and without discomfort outside the bubbles.

In return, Kymri enlarged a little on what he knew of the history of Noi Lantis—which was not much. And it was so mixed up with folklore and legend that not until some time later was she able to appreciate its significance. In the beginning, according to Kymri, long before the founding of Noi Lantis, there had been many cities in lands where there were no forests and where the skies were often clear and the stars could be seen at night. That was the time of the sky beasts, the great plague sent by the divine joker Godfred to chasten mankind. Presently, the sky beasts ate up all the cities until there was hardly anyone left alive. At which point Godfred ceased to be amused, for few were left to appreciate his humour.

So, after some thought, Godfred decided to allow a new city to flourish, provided the men who lived in it remained suitably appreciative of the divine humour of life and death. So he caused the Fathers to rise up out of the very earth of the forest, and women came with them. And together, and with true appreciation of the humour of Godfred, they began to build a city and beget children to live in it. Because the Fathers remained devout, Godfred was pleased to endow them with some of the skills and mysteries of the cities that had flourished in lands across the oceans. He endowed the people of Noi Lantis with electrics, generators, wire messages. He gave medicine and tools, and clepsydras that men might measure the passing of time. He gave the secret of moving pictures for amusement, and the art of embalming sound so that a man's voice could be heard across the years.

Mirlena and Kymri talked until the darkness waned and until it was about time to rouse the others and prepare for another day's trek. They talked about much, but about nothing connected directly with themselves. This time, the darkness had not magically made them of one race. It had pushed them apart, reminding them of differences—and of the embarrassment of a shared but fortunately brief insanity.

The third day's trek was fairly uneventful. Garl Sinjorge twisted his ankle and slowed the party down. Otherwise, they might have reached Noi Lantis before darkness on the third day. Garl sacrificed his pride at last by allowing Kymri to carry his rucksack. Kymri also showed him how to use a springy but not uncomfortable crutch made out of a slender piece of soft wood.

In the last watch of the last night, Kymri alluded once only to the passion that he and Mirlena had shared, it seemed to her now, not in any real sense but only in a dreamlike frenzy—a discharge, she told herself grimly, of surplus adrenalin inspired by a snake that never struck.

"You have not forgotten?" asked Kymri quietly.

"I have not forgotten." In the darkness, she knew that he was looking at her, and was pleased that she could be relaxed and without fear.

"It is something not to forget," he said. Then he added obscurely: "It was the pleasure of Godfred. And who shall know if Godfred destroys or creates."

Late in the morning of the fourth day, they came to the walled city of Noi Lantis.

Looking across the cleared land at its towers and domes, Mirlena had the feeling that the journey from the sloop had been not a physical journey but a long downward fall through time. And, looking at Noi Lantis, she had a premonition that an even longer fall, through the very floor of history, lay ahead.

CHAPTER TWENTY-ONE

Urlanrey, king of Noi Lantis, sat formally on the dragon throne in the great Sun Chamber of the palace. Behind him stood seven officers of the Pryterguard. On a stool to the left of the throne sat Numon, the First Consul; on a stool to the right of the throne sat Kymriso, the Second Consul, who was also Kymri's mother; and on the steps leading up to the throne sat Stasius, priest and Lord of the Generators.

The Sun Chamber was, in fact, a great glass dome set on top of the highest stone tower in the Palace. The light passing through innumerable tinted glass panes was transformed into a rich amber, bathing everyone and everything in the circular chamber in a darkly golden glow.

Kymri stood before the steps to the throne with the four Martian negroes, upon whom all eyes in the chamber were fixed, it seemed, unwaveringly. He had told his story and had been graciously interrupted by Urlanrey only twice. On the first occasion the king remarked that it was fortunate that the original sky beasts were extinct since it was certain that, despite Kymri's undoubted valour, they could not be slain by mere mortals; and on the second occasion, he observed mildly that it was indeed fortunate that Kymri had brought witnesses, who could confirm that he had left the surface of the Earth for a time, since man had not yet developed the means to fly.

During the course of his story—particularly when he was recounting the destruction of the probe—Kymri glanced at Kymriso once or twice, as if to seek approval for his actions. But Kymriso, still a strikingly beautiful woman although she was nearly forty years old, wore not the aspect of a mother but of the king's Second Consul. She gazed gravely and with curiosity at Kymri, but with no sign of recognition, almost as if he were as much a stranger as the Martian negroes.

Kord Vengel was distinctly uneasy, and his agitation was apparent to everyone in the Sun Chamber. When confronted only by Kymri he had learned to contain his phobia to some extent. But in the presence of so many white people, he was bitterly unhappy. He wanted either to run or to destroy, and kept having to tell himself that it was practical to do neither.

While Kymri was talking, Kord continually fingered his needle pistol nervously. The officers of the Pryterguard, sensing the needle pistol to be a weapon, held their own short javelins more tightly. The king gave no sign of being aware of this tension.

After Kymri had finished speaking, there was a brief silence. Stasius the priest coughed, attracting the king's attention, and seemed to incline his head slightly, as if answering an unspoken question.

The king rose from the dragon throne and spoke to his guests.

"Strangers, the young man Kymri—a person yet lacking in wisdom, perhaps, if not in courage—has brought you from the forest to Noi Lantis. He says that you have come in peace and that presently you will depart in peace. He says also that though you speak a strange language some of you understand our tongue. This is welcome news to us and enables us to joyfully offer the hospitality of our city.

"No doubt with the pardonable exaggeration of youth, the young man who brought you says that you are people of great and varied skills, that you have voyaged to this world from another in a vessel of the night that can traverse the gaps between the stars.

"This, to us of Noi Lantis, is a strange story indeed; and you must forgive us if we find it difficult to accept or comprehend. We are told that your vessel now rests on top of the sky, but that you came down to the forest in a smaller craft. We would find it more easy to accept this remarkable fact if the craft were available for inspection; but we are told that though it came down to the forest, many kaymets away, it has now returned to the sky with no one to guide it.

"That you are not people of the forest, there can be no doubt. In the course of time, the people of Noi Lantis have ventured far into the forest and even beyond it. They have encountered desert and a great ocean; but they have discovered no other city, no other people. Nor, in the long history of Noi Lantis, has there been any knowledge of any living race whose skins are black such as yours.

"However, according to the scriptures, there were once many cities scattered in the far places of the Earth; and it is said that in these cities there lived people whose skins were dark as well as people whose skins were pale. It is known that the cities were destroyed by sky beasts, according to the humour of Godfred. But perhaps not all the cities were destroyed, or not all of their people. The descendants of the survivors, if inspired to journey far from their own land, would no doubt desire to be prudent until they discovered whether any other race they encountered were warlike or peaceful.

"I do not ask you at this time to make the story I have heard more clear, or to declare yourselves in any way that might seem to harm your own security. I ask you only as my guests to accept the laws of this city. We of Noi Lantis have little taste for violence. The forest breeds violence. Let the city breed understanding. I have required that no man's hands or weapons shall be raised against you, as I hope that your hands and weapons shall be raised against none.

"Friendship we would have, knowledge we would have. Let

that be the sum of our traffic. Chambers have been prepared for you in the Temple of Godfred. My priests will tell you where you may or may not pass. We will speak again, when you have rested."

Mirlena looked at Kord Vengel, the only other Martian who could hope to understand what the king had said, and thank him for his courtesy. But Kord was evidently too involved in his own emotional reaction to be able to pay much rational attention to the king's words or to make a suitable reply. He was fidgetting a great deal and constantly looking behind him, as if he expected them to be attacked from the rear or to have their retreat cut off.

So Mirlena took it upon herself to thank Urlanrey for his kindness. "I and my companions are very grateful," she said, "that you will allow us to stay a little time in Noi Lantis. We came to you peacefully, although, as you see, we carry weapons, and we hope to leave peacefully. We hope also to learn something of your way of life and, in exchange, to tell you about ourselves."

The king looked at her, puzzled. "In your country it is customary for a woman to speak for men?" His glance flickered briefly to Kord Vengel, whom he had suspected of being the leader of the party.

Mirlena smiled. "In our world, women share tasks equally with men and also hold high office. But I speak for my companions chiefly because I understand your language better than they . . . Though it may be hard to believe, it is true what the young man, Kymri, has told you. We do not come from any city of Earth. We come from a world that is called Mars. It is warmed by the same sun as this world of yours, but it is many thousands of thousands of kaymets away in the sky. The journey is hazardous and costly. It can only be made in a special ship that needs great skills, great patience and much labour to build. It needs great knowledge of metals and their uses, and knowledge of electrics and substances that make tremendous heat. Long ago, there were other ships that travelled between Earth and Mars; but this is the first time the journey has been made for two thousand years."

"Others of your kind will follow?" enquired the king pertinently.

Mirlena was as honest as she dared to be. "Others may come later," she admitted, "but because of the difficulties of the journey, this will not happen for a long time. First, we ourselves must return to Mars and report what we have seen. If we are able to report that the people of Noi Lantis are our friends, then the people of Mars will be very happy."

"Is there a great city, such as Noi Lantis, on this world you call Mars?"

Tactically, Mirlena made a mistake. "There are many cities on Mars, some much larger than Noi Lantis."

"And each of these cities is governed by its own king?"

"There are no kings on Mars. There is one person whom we call President. Helped by advisers, the President controls the destiny of all the cities of Mars."

The king was silent for a while. Stasius the priest got up from the steps, approached the dragon throne and whispered in Urlanrey's ear. The king shook his head slightly. Then he turned to Kymri.

"Kymri op Kymriso, by the whim of Godfred you have brought strangers to our city, bearing tales of great wonder. Stay with these people of the dark skins, see to their comfort and their needs. Show them what they may lawfully see and, with the guidance of Stasius, help them to learn what they may lawfully know." He smiled faintly. "But remember also that you are of Noi Lantis, not of this place called Mars."

Kymri knelt. Urlanrey gave a sign that the audience was over. The officers of the Pryterguard muttered among themselves. Stasius came to conduct the visitors to the Temple of Godfred.

CHAPTER TWENTY-TWO

The Temple of Godfred was the largest building or complex of buildings in Noi Lantis, larger even than the Dragon Palace of Urlanrey. As Kymri and the Martians left the palace, led by Stasius and a courtesy escort of spear-carrying guards, Mirlena looked in wonder at the ring of finely carved stone dragons that squatted like great armoured sentinels round the stone-faced halls and towers. She had thought that such beasts could only be mythical creatures, and was amazed when Kymri explained that komdeldo dragons—for such they were called—were the fiercest creatures of the forest. The larger ones grew to the height and three times the length of a man. Frequently, and with an almost seasonal blood-lust, they hunted in packs, annihilating everything in their path. But, at times also, they were so placid and gentle that a child could stroke them with safety. Combining terrible power and sudden gentleness, they were fitting symbols for the authority of the king.

Kord Vengel, apparently, was now managing to control the signs of intense stress that he had displayed during the audience with the king. Perhaps the fact that he had actually emerged from the palace alive had convinced him—temporarily, at least—that the people of Noi Lantis represented no immediate threat. Despite their superior weapons, it would have been possible for the Martians to have been killed in the Sun Chamber. They had been surrounded by people, and there would have been little room to manoeuvre or use their arms without endangering themselves. But all had passed off reasonably well, and Kord was satisfied enough with the reception to relax a little. As the party was taken to the Temple of Godfred, he was even able to make a few rather feeble jokes about his comparatively barbaric hosts.

The Temple of Godfred was more than a temple. It was a school, a university, a gymnasium, a scientific institution, a hospital, a court and a political forum all combined. It was, in fact, the cultural centre of Noi Lantis. From it came all law and learning, upon it was bestowed almost a quarter of the entire wealth—reckoned not in artificial currency but in the real currency of food, resources and labour—of Noi Lantis.

Before he took them to their quarters, Stasius, priest and Lord of the Generators, took his visitors upon a conducted tour of his extensive domain, perhaps seeking to impress these people who claimed to employ machines more wonderful than the mind of man could devise.

First, he showed them the laboratories and workshops, where anodynes and curatives were compounded in an atmosphere as religious, as mystical and as fanatical as any developed by the ancient medieval alchemists of Earth. The priests sat on high stools at long wooden benches, surrounded by primitive glassware, pestles, mortars, herbs, salts and odd little gas burners with which they heated their medicinal compounds. Each priest was attended by a small boy, who moved and arranged apparatus for him as well as fetching ingredients that were not within easy reach.

From the laboratories, Stasius took his guests to the acolyte workshops where novice priests, fresh from castration, were learning to wind their first armatures or construct their first electro-magnets.

By the time the Martians had inspected the hospital—where Mirlena sensed that more patients were dying than living—the law-makers' cells and the Hall of Argument, dusk was already falling. Stasius, as Lord of the Generators, issued a command to one of his attendants. Presently, rudimentary carbon-filament lamps flickered into life and light; and the Martians were aware of a subdued humming wherever they went.

The last place that Stasius showed them—and the only building they did not enter—before he escorted them to the rooms that had been assigned to them in the Hall of the King's Retreat, was the tower of the Abode of the Dead.

It was the most curious and the most interesting structure in the whole of Noi Lantis. It stood in the temple courtyard, and was the tallest building in the entire city. The Martians were only allowed to inspect it briefly and by twilight; but it seemed to them to be totally out of keeping with the rest of the architecture they had seen.

It was a slender, functional tower. It appeared to be made not of stone but of concrete. It was topped—as were all the other towers of the city—by a glass-panelled dome. But this dome seemed different than the rest. It looked more like an observatory.

Kord Vengel overcame his repugnance, his feeling of natural superiority and his prejudice to speak to Stasius for the first time.

"You have told us that this tower is called the Abode of the Dead. Why should there be a chamber at the top where it is possible to see further than from any other place in your city?"

"Sir," said Stasius evenly, "the dead who are not our dead, and are not wholly dead by reason of never having wholly lived, have eyes. The chamber you see is their window upon the world. They have used it only five times during my lifetime. What their purpose is, I know not. But they have given us much wisdom, and I am content." He paused, then looked directly and sombrely at Kord Vengel. "The Abode of the Dead, which, as you see is not guarded, is holy ground. Urlanrey, the king, myself and the First and Second Consuls only are privileged to pass through its doorway. This we do not lightly. But sometimes the need is great. As Lord of the Generators, I have accompanied Urlanrey and

Numon twice to the Abode of the Dead. I have no desire to venture there again . . . I believe that the guests of the king will respect the sanctity of this tower. Indeed, were it otherwise, death might come swiftly, though the life of a guest is more valued than the life of a first son."

Inwardly, Kord Vengel raged at the implied threat. He, an intelligent and superior being, was not to be intimidated by the threat of a primitive white savage. But there would be time—yes, indeed there would be time—to smash the tabus and the absurd affectations of this primitive race. Perhaps, in the end, they need not be exterminated. Perhaps, if Mars decided to set up a permanent base and raw materials production centre on this planet, the Noi Lantians could be used for slave labour.

He smiled at the thought. That would be poetic justice with a vengeance. He smiled at the thought, and smiled also at Stasius the priest.

CHAPTER TWENTY-THREE

The Hall of the King's Retreat consisted of a large self-contained suite of rooms together with its own kitchen, to which the king, accompanied sometimes by his consuls or favourites, would retire for regular periods during each year. During such periods, he would confer with his law-makers, administrators, 'scientific' and spiritual advisers about the long and short term problems facing Noi Lantis and the measures that could be taken to deal with them. Symbolically, while he stayed in the Temple of Godfred, he submitted to the authority of Stasius, as Priest of Godfred and Lord of the Generators. In practice, he was regularly entering a primitive university for refresher courses in all subjects; it being only fitting that the king should be as wise and as knowledgeable as any of his subjects. Urlanrey also stayed in the King's Retreat during the temple games, at the end of which he would award the Crown of Invincibility to the victorious athlete who would then be further honoured by occupying the dragon throne for one day.

The chambers in the King's Retreat were simply but comfortably furnished. Skin rugs abounded on the floors and the dried moss mattresses of the beds, carbon filament lamps flickered erratically from brackets on the stone walls, and an oil lamp burned in a niche in the wall of each room in case the electrics failed. Each room also contained pleasingly shaped wooden tables and chairs, and the broad yellow-paned windows were covered by plain, dark curtains.

Each Martian was offered a private chamber. Kord Vengel was of the opinion that, to defeat any attempt at treachery, all four ought to share the same chamber, taking turns to watch throughout the night. Garl Sinjorge was agreeable to this; but Mirlena and Rudlan Others were not—for different reasons. Mirlena was weary of Kord Vengel's company and his constant assumption that everybody was against him, and Rudlan desired a privacy that, if the occasion arose, he might share intimately with Mirlena. In the end, Kord Vengel and Garl Sinjorge decided to share a room, while Mirlena and Rudlan had separate rooms.

Stasius waited patiently as his guests conferred in their own language. He accepted their decisions without comment, and proudly showed them how each room contained a wonderful method of summoning an attendant by electrics. All you had to do was close a simple knife-switch—so!—and a priest would come running. He demonstrated this wonder several times, as much, evidently, for his own satisfaction as for that of his guests.

Urlanrey had commanded that Kymri remain with the Martians during their stay; but as he was not an honoured guest he was not given one of the royal chambers. Instead he was assigned to a priest-secretary's chamber, small and poorly furnished, recessed in a corner of the main hall and next to a similar chamber which would always be occupied by the two priest-attendants on duty.

When Stasius had seen his guests settled in their accommodation, he ordered fruit, cold meat, pastries and water and wine to be brought for them, saying that, after their journey through the forest, their audience with the king and the tour of the temple, they must be hungry and tired. He assumed, therefore, that they would wish to refresh themselves in their own fashion and sleep before desiring further attentions from their hosts.

The priest spoke formally and courteously. Mirlena was thankful for his consideration. Again she spoke for the Martians. She told Stasius that she and her companions welcomed his kindness, that they were indeed tired but that on the following day they hoped to see again many of the wonderful things they had been shown. She said also that during their visit the Martians hoped to be able to demonstrate something of their own achievements.

Stasius listened to her words without comment. When she had finished, he bowed slightly, then signed to Kymri to follow him.

As they walked away from the royal chambers, down the long hall that was lit by carbon lamps and that echoed the muted throb of the dynamos, he turned to Kymri and said: "Boy, in bringing these strangers, you have brought us a pretty problem. Already, I perceive that the ways and attitudes of our people can never be the same again."

Kymri was already feeling depressed, and did not need Stasius to add to his depression. "Sir, I had little choice," he answered gloomily. "They are people of great skills, and I do not doubt that they could have found Noi Lantis themselves. Was it not better that I lead them here as a friend?"

Stasius did not answer the question. Instead, he said softly: "A little knowledge is dangerous. Great knowledge also is dangerous. If their story has any substance, these people of Mars have knowledge that makes our knowledge as that of children . . . It must be considered whether it is not better to kill them."

Kymri shook his head. "They have companions with powerful weapons resting now in their ship that sits on top of the sky. Kill these, and the next visitors to Noi Lantis may be fire and death. Their power is such that they can visit such things upon us even as they sail the oceans of the night."

"Truly, the humour of Godfred is awesome and disturbing," observed the priest. He gazed at Kymri intently; "You would swear that what you have told the king of your own part in this venture is exactly true and not, perhaps, stretched somewhat by the imagination of a young man seeking importance in the eyes of his people?"

"It is the truth. I wish it were not."

"Black faces and black bodies," mused the priest. "What if there is also much blackness in their hearts?" He sighed. "If we do not kill them, or they and their companions do not kill us, we may end by serving them. A sorry choice."

Then, as he passed through the great doorway in the Hall of the King's Retreat, Stasius said: "Watch them well, Kymri op Kymriso. Watch them closely. Your own part in the drama is such that your prospect of achieving a ripe age seems less good than it once was."

Kymri watched the tall, commanding figure of the Lord of the Generators, almost bird-like in his long green gown of office, pass down the stone-walled corridor, lit by the flickering of electrics.

With Stasius, he had never known whether his actions or ambitions were approved or disapproved. Which was disconcerting. Because the priest was one of the two men who might be Kymri's father.

CHAPTER TWENTY-FOUR

After Stasius had left them, the four Martians held a brief conference in the room that was shared by Kord Vengel and Garl Sinjorge. They were all very tired with the events of the day, and relaxed gratefully on the skin rugs, feeling the relentless gravity of Earth tugging endlessly at their exhausted bodies.

Kord gestured at the food and drink that had been brought. "I am not going to eat any of that. I shall keep to our concentrates, and I would advise the rest of you to do the same."

The food seemed appetizing enough, and Garl Sinjorge licked his lips. "You think it may cause digestive problems? We ought to be able to deal with it." He smiled. "After all, our ancestors on Earth didn't have any problems . . . But I suppose there is the possibility that new strains of bugs might have developed."

Mirlena said evenly: "I think Kord is more concerned with drugs than bugs . . . I shall at least sample my food—when I have the energy."

"I'm concerned with every possibility," snapped Kord with some irritation. "I would like to survive this little venture, and I propose to take as many precautions as I can. One doesn't know what these people are thinking or how they react to us; and, in any case, tackling a three-course meal of native food is just asking for trouble.

"There is also the question of watches," went on Kord. "We ought to stand watches throughout the night—in fact, throughout every night while we are here."

Rudlan Others smiled. "I see no point in it; and, personally, I'm really too tired . . . If these people mean mischief, there are dozens of ways in which they could deal with us, despite our nasty little scientific toys." He looked at the weapons, which Kord had laid out like a small armoury by the side of his bed. "They won't do us any good, Kord. Certainly, we can eliminate a few hundred of the populace if need be. But before the sloop could get us back into orbit, these people would find a way of dealing with us. They are not unintelligent—and they know their environment, we don't . . . No, I think we must take them on trust, just as they are doing with us."

Kord Vengel snorted. "Trust! What trust can there be between black Martians and white savages?"

"As much as we care to make," said Mirlena. "Rudlan is right. We have to assume friendship. Otherwise we go crazy with fear and ineffective precautions." She yawned. "I am going to my room. I shall lock myself in—yes, I noticed that convenience— eat my poisoned food, neglect to look under the bed, and fall asleep before the secret panel opens." She giggled. "If I am still alive in the morning, I shall want to find out a lot more about savages who treat aliens with hospitality, use electricity, and bleed sick people with nasty little things called leeches."

"You will be haunted by ghosts," said Rudlan with a grin, "from the Abode of the Dead. Perhaps they are the secret weapon of the terrestrials."

"Ah, yes, the Abode of the Dead," said Kord Vengel thoughtfully. "We must dwell upon that little mystery. One thing is sure; it is not what that priest says it is . . . Yes, that is something to investigate."

Mirlena yawned again. "Tomorrow," she said. "Our neural

circuits are already overloaded. My professional advice is that we all rest as much as possible—otherwise we shall solve everybody's problems by simply destroying ourselves . . . Good night. Bear in mind that we are supposed to talk with the king again . . . I hope, Kord, that you are not going to be as ferocious as last time. You made the royal guard very nervous."

With that parting shot, Mirlena left the chamber and returned to her own.

Meanwhile, Kymri was settling himself in the small priest-secretary's chamber that he had been given. He had thought about visiting the Martians to see that they were comfortable and had what they needed; but then he decided against it. They would probably wish to talk among themselves for a while; and in any case, they had been shown how to summon an attendant.

He looked at the food that had been placed in the chamber for him and realized that he was very hungry indeed. He had just sampled a slice or two of the meat when there was a knock at the door, and a yellow-robed novice priest entered.

"To Kymri op Kymriso, greetings from Mirlena Stroza, guest of the king and of the Lord of the Generators," he said formally. "I am bidden to say that the person named desires your advice and assistance. The humour of Godfred be with you."

"Such humour," responded Kymri automatically, "lying benevolently upon us all." He looked at his meal regretfully. "I cannot remember when I was last offered such food as this; but first I must do my duty as the king commanded." He left his own small chamber and walked down the Hall of the King's Retreat.

When he had entered Mirlena's chamber, she barred the door after him. Kymri looked at her, surprised.

"I do not want us to be interrupted," she said. "My companions, though tired, are restless. They do not trust you, Kymri and—" she hesitated "—and, as you know, they might easily be angered to find us alone together."

Kymri smiled. "But now we are in my country, and their anger may matter less than it did . . . What did you want of me?"

"Companionship, information, assurance."

He was puzzled. "The companionship of your own people is surely—"

"It is not what I want," she interrupted. "Do not be stupid, Kymri. It is not what I want, and I need say no more." She gestured towards the food. "It looks good. But there is far too much for me to eat alone. Will you join me?"

Kymri was suddenly amused. "I do not think the food is poisoned. Urlanrey has more direct methods, if he cares to use them."

"I did not think it was poisoned. My stomach may find it a little strange, but I think that will be the worst that will happen. Now, pour some wine—as much as you would for a woman of your own kind—and tell me what we should eat first."

Mirlena rested on the broad mattress of the guest bed, while Kymri poured the wine and described the taste of the pears and pineapples and cherries and the pressed beef and the spiced sausage and the sweet and savoury pastries. Presently, Mirlena sipped the dark red wine, feeling a delicious warmth surging through her limbs; and Kymri showed her how to nibble alternately at the hot and cold pears to add strange and fascinating flavours to the meat that she ate.

There were no knives and forks, but there were finger bowls and napkins. Mirlena watched how Kymri ate his food and emulated him. For a while, they ate in silence.

The wine was like an elixir. With every sip, new fire and energy seemed to be pumped into her body. It was not that she felt drunk, but as if fatigue and tension were dissolving away, as if her mind was becoming abnormally clear, as if some tremendous discovery was about to filter into her thoughts.

"What kind of wine is this?"

Kymri sipped from his own glass appreciatively. "You and your companions are honoured. It is the king's own wine, made from ling berries—very small fruit that are wild and hard to find —and crushed ants. The priests of Godfred distil and fortify it. I have tasted it only three times before, during the temple games." He laughed. "They say that a flagon of it will restore

123

the dead to life."

The ache had gone from Mirlena's limbs. She felt that, even under the terrible G force of Earth, she could dance lightly and effortlessly.

"It is certainly restoring me to life," said Mirlena. "On this world of yours, Kymri, my body feels very heavy—much heavier than on Mars . . . That is why all of us, who are among the strongest of our own race, cannot easily do the simple things that you Earth people do. For you it is nothing to run and jump, and to walk many kaymets in a day. For us, it is completely exhausting." She smiled. "If we ever set up a base on Earth, we shall have to persuade you and your people to do the heavy work for us." Then suddenly she realized the implications of what she had said, and the smile left her face.

Kymri gazed at her calmly. "Do you think that we who are white would willingly become slaves to a race of black strangers from across the sky?"

"I did not mean it that way."

"Perhaps not. But others will . . . Do you believe that Kord Vengel does not want to make slaves of us? I think there may be many Kord Vengels in your world. Such is the humour of Godfred."

"Let us not talk about it," she said. "I do not want to talk about it. The problem is one that cannot arise for many years."

"So much the better. We of Noi Lantis will have time to dwell on the prospect—and prepare ourselves." He smiled. "Even to the all-powerful Martians, the price of slaves may be somewhat high."

Mirlena drank more wine in a desperate effort to restore the euphoria. "There is something I wish to know, Kymri. It is important. I want you to tell me truly and exactly what you think of black skin, black bodies, black people."

He was disconcerted, and did not answer for a moment or two. Then he said carefully: "I think they are very strange."

She seemed disappointed. "Is that all?"

"No. That is not all . . . At first, I was greatly afraid. Then, as time passed and I was a prisoner in your vessel, the fear changed into hatred. I hated the broad noses, the thick lips, the flattened faces, the strange sounds you made, the white smiles, even the curious scent of your bodies. But such hatred either drives a man mad or eats itself away. I reasoned that, through your eyes, we who have light skins, sharp noses, thin lips and different body smells must also seem horrible." He laughed. "Great is the humour of Godfred. Presently, I thought I was indeed going mad, for I could perceive that black bodies had their own forms of beauty. I noticed this most when we were in orbit, and there was lightness in all things, and your people could move with grace . . . Here on Earth, you are ungainly once more. But I know this is because of the weight your bodies have to bear." He looked at her directly. "Here, on Earth also, I learned that darkness conceals both blackness and whiteness. So I lay with a woman and found much pleasure—doubtless to the amusement of Godfred."

Mirlena returned his gaze, and found difficulty in speaking. "At first, I was ashamed," she said softly. "At first, I was greatly ashamed and afraid . . . But there is a language that is older than any of the sounds we care to make. Perhaps we do not use it enough . . . Kymri, do you wish to lie with a woman once more?"

"Yes, but not as a savage—or as a slave."

Mirlena took his hand and guided it to the zip-lock of her trek suit.

"Not even as the ghost of an owner of black slaves," she murmured incomprehensibly. "Only as a man . . . Do we need the darkness this time, Kymri?"

He shook his head. "Let us look upon each other. Let us look upon each other as we are."

CHAPTER TWENTY-FIVE

Kymri did not stay the night with Mirlena. After they had made love, they lay close together, talking for a while, marvelling at the strangeness and the familiarity of each other's bodies, rejoicing in the after-glow of sexual frenzy.

It had been different in the light. It had been different and indescribably more exciting. All the time that they had touched and loved, all the time the white flesh lay sheathed in the black, they had looked at each other, as if seeing for the first time. Even through the thundery mists of orgasm, they looked at each other, wondering, hardly knowing what they saw.

When they were sensible enough to be able to think again, one thing was clear: the shame had gone. There was no shame in white desiring black, in black desiring white. They knew now that there had only been shame in the sense of shame.

But, though shame had gone, it was replaced by fear, by depression, by profound sadness. They were enemies who desired each other, they were friends who must lose each other. They were, above all, creatures of two sadly different worlds.

Dr. Mirlena Stroza, educated black Martian, psychologist, interplanetary explorer, woman of considerable intellectual power, had established a private bond—call it love, call it desire, call it perversion—with a primitive, white, earth-bound male. She had reversed two thousand years of conditioning, she had ignored differences of culture and intelligence simply in order to hazard the safety of the expedition by indulging in a personal whim. Call it madness.

Mirlena knew that there were a hundred reasons why Kymri should be kept at a distance; and in the end there would probably be some excellent reasons why he and his kind should be enslaved or killed. But all this seemed irrelevant. All that mattered was that she had lain with him, that she had derived great pleasure from the experience—and that she was a stupid and dangerous fool.

As they touched and stroked and explored each other, Kymri sensed the conflict in her mind.

"Be easy, sweet one, little one," he soothed. "The savage will not betray his princess of the night. We stretch out a hand to each other for a moment; but we are separated by the great deeps of space, by the mysteries of strange machines, by all the thoughts you have that I can neither share nor understand. It is enough that we have touched each other. Presently, you will go your way and I will go mine." He smiled. "None shall know how these two enemies conducted their battle. We will leave your people and my people to the pleasure of their mutual fears . . . I must return to my own chamber now. It would be wise."

When he left, there were tears in Mirlena's eyes.

Despite the pleasures of the senses, Kymri's own spirit felt heavy. Such was the humour of Godfred.

CHAPTER TWENTY-SIX

The following morning Urlanrey sent a messenger to the Temple of Godfred to say that the king desired to speak with the black woman alone. Urlanrey was old and conservative in his attitudes. It had offended his sense of propriety that Mirlena had been the one to speak when her three companions were men. But he was astute enough to sense the undercurrents of tension that had pervaded the Sun Chamber, and sensed also that it might be possible to obtain—or exchange—more valuable information if he talked to Mirlena in an atmosphere of privacy and informality.

The messenger came directly to Mirlena while she was taking breakfast with Rudlan Others. She was amazed at the request; but after a moment's thought she accepted it. Then she swore Rudlan Others to secrecy. If Kord Vengel learned of the invitation, he would see it only as part of a scheme to divide the Martians and deal with them separately.

Rudlan was uneasy at the thought of Mirlena going anywhere alone; but she laughed at his fears, pointing out that they had come to Noi Lantis to learn about its culture and people, and that if all their actions were to be limited by irrational fear they should never have undertaken the project. Reluctantly, Rudlan agreed to say nothing.

Presently, they were joined by Kord Vengel and Garl Sinjorge.

"This fellow Stasius, Lord of the Children's Toys, is going to give us another conducted tour," said Kord, with a grin. "For a savage, he is polite enough—not that one trusts him, of course—but it amuses me that he presumes to intelligence . . . You are supporting a lost cause, Mirlena. These people are regressing so fast that in a few more generations they will resort to witchcraft and sacrifice . . . Did you sleep well?"

"Well enough," she answered evenly. "But I'm not coming on your conducted tour, Kord. I'm too tired physically. Please make my excuses."

"What are you going to do?"

"Stay in my room and rest for a while."

"You can't be left alone."

"She won't be," said Rudlan. "I can't come with you, either. I have to make contact with Streven Luse when the ship comes over the horizon. Conditions here are pretty awful for transmission. There's a lot of stuff to get back to Streven, so I shall probably have to wait for a second orbit."

Kord Vengel frowned. "I don't like this splitting up. It's dangerous."

"Everything we are doing could be dangerous," observed Mirlena. "I think the risks are acceptable. Now, stop worrying. I shall be in my room; and I presume Rudlan will want to use the courtyard. We can contact each other quickly, if need be."

"Where is your pet savage?"

"I don't know. In the little room they gave him, I expect."

"Good. He can come along with us." He laughed grimly. "He'll do as a hostage—along with Stasius."

.   .   .

Urlanrey had abandoned his ornate robes of office and was wearing a simple white tunic. He did not receive Mirlena in the Sun Chamber but in the sitting-room of his private apartment in the Palace. Then he dismissed his attendants and the officer of the Pryterguard who had conducted Mirlena into the room.

"My daughter," said Urlanrey with odd familiarity, "I trust that Stasius, Lord of the Generators, has fulfilled his duty, that you have eaten a sufficiency and rested well, and that we of Noi Lantis need not be ashamed of our hospitality."

"I and my companions are grateful for your kindness. We shall speak with pleasure of the hospitality of Noi Lantis when we return to our own world."

"Ah, yes. The very point I wish to raise . . . Do not misunderstand me, Lady Mirlena, but it is necessary to know how long you will stay, how soon you must go."

"I understand. We should be able to stay for five more days. We may be able to stay a day or two longer. It depends, I think, how and where our companions who sail the vessel in the sky hope to meet us . . . But if our presence is inconvenient, we will be happy to leave at your bidding."

Urlanrey looked shocked. "We do not turn away guests—even though their origins may be obscure."

Mirlena smiled. "My father," she said with subtle emphasis, "I think we understand each other. You believe, do you not, that we are from another city beyond the forest, beyond the desert and beyond the ocean?"

Urlanrey smiled. "It is easier upon my mind than tales of vessels that can cross the gaps between the stars . . . The young man Kymri—for whom I have some personal affection—possesses great imagination. Being inexperienced, he is also easily misled. It is in the nature of youth to describe a breeze as a whirlwind . . . I can forgive his misunderstandings."

"Kymri op Kymriso speaks the truth."

Urlanrey raised an eyebrow. "Then you hold to this story of a world on the other side of the sky?"

"Please believe me. It is so."

Urlanrey was silent for a while. Then he said: "You black ones must be a powerful race indeed. What is your purpose here? Why have you come to Noi Lantis?"

"We did not know of the existence of Noi Lantis. But now that we have found it, we wish to learn as much as possible about its people and the wisdom of those who govern it."

"Others will come after, as you said?"

"I believe so. But it will not be for a long time."

Urlanrey was again silent for a time. "I have read the scriptures. It is written that when two races meet, bloodshed must follow, for one will seek to dominate the other . . . Why should I not have you and your companions killed now, to discourage those who would come after?"

Mirlena shrugged. How could she explain things to this feudal king who, despite his intelligence, lived in a world of ignorance?

"Our deaths would prove costly," she said. "I think you could destroy us without suffering too much from the terrible weapons we possess. But our comrades in the vessel in the sky have even more terrible weapons. Without setting foot in Noi Lantis, they could destroy the city and all who live in it . . . I beg of you, do not put them to the test. It is as I have said . . . If you wish, I will show you the power of the small weapons that we have brought with us. But I would do so with a great sadness. Is it right that we should do so? I believe that it would be dreadfully wrong."

"My daughter, you have some wisdom. May we dare to believe that others of your race share that wisdom?"

Mirlena looked at Urlanrey, seeing not a feudal monarch but a man groping in darkness—a man seeking the best solution for his people. She felt a great compassion.

"I must speak the truth, whatever it brings. There are others of my race who think as I do, who believe that violence and bloodshed are the worst afflictions of mankind. But there are many who do not. Long ago, our ancestors also lived on Earth, at a time when the white races, who lived in many cities in many countries, were proud and strong. It was a time, also, when men had learned to build great ships to cross the sky to distant worlds. The black race and the white race quarrelled; and the quarrel resulted in a dreadful war which destroyed cities and people and almost the Earth itself. Some of my race were fortunate to be able to sail in the great ships to the world we call Mars. There, believing that all the white people of Earth were dead, they built a new civilization. Some time ago, they decided to send an expedition to Earth, which was supposed to be a dead world, to seek rare metals and substances that we of Mars cannot obtain easily . . .

"Now that we have discovered that Earth is not dead, I do not know what will happen. Many people on Mars still think of the white people of Earth with great bitterness. But I know, too, that there will be many who wish to hold out the hand of friendship."

Mirlena looked at Urlanrey helplessly, aware of the turmoil in his mind. She could hardly blame him if, in the simplicity of his reasoning and the confusion created by realities that he could not comprehend, he thought it best to kill these strangers who threatened the tranquillity of centuries.

Urlanrey sighed. "I could wish that we had never met, that your companions in the sky vessel had encountered some overwhelming disaster. But I suppose that it would not have solved the problem. Later, others would have come . . . So, perhaps I must take what consolation I can from the story of the dragon, the man and the condasnake."

"Tell me the story."

"Once, a wise man was wandering in the forest, when he encountered a komdo dragon, perhaps the most fearsome creature there is. From the colour of the dragon, the wise man knew that it was in hunting season. If he turned to run, it would outrun him. If he attacked it with his spear it would destroy him. Also, he had noticed that, in any case, his only line of retreat was blocked by the largest condasnake he had ever seen. Faced with such perils, he decided to do nothing at all, reasoning that only a fool would assist at his own destruction, inevitable though the destruction may be.

"The dragon was accustomed to striking terror or rage into the hearts of all living creatures it encountered, and could not understand why the man should stand there calmly, awaiting his end. It approached him. It stamped on the ground till the trees shook, it roared, it threshed its tail about. Still the man did nothing.

"The hungry condasnake, which had been stalking the man, was diverted by the antics of the dragon. Especially when the dragon carelessly stamped on the snake's tail. Immediately, the condasnake struck, coiling itself around the dragon. There followed a brief and bloody battle, during which the wise man continued to stand still, marvelling at the savagery of the creatures locked in combat. Eventually as the snake crushed the bones and heart of the dragon, the dying dragon bit the head off the snake. With both these fearsome creatures dead, the wise man was free to go in peace . . .

"Let us hope that the dragon of hatred and the condasnake of distrust destroy each other; for if they do not, there is little to hope for anyone in your world or in mine."

Suddenly, Mirlena felt humble. "I am glad that you have told me this story. I, in turn, shall tell it to my people."

Urlanrey gave her a tired smile. "There is something else that should be remembered by both our races. The colour of the skin is less important than the spirit which moves it."

.   .   .

Amid a group of interested priests, Rudlan Others set up his small transceiver in the main courtyard of the Temple of God-fred. As he was unable to explain to them in their own language what he was doing, they had to interpret his behaviour as well as they could. The transceiver, with its telescopic aerial, though finely made, did not seem to them to be an impressive piece of equipment; and the fact that the black visitor spoke to it a great deal inclined them to the view that there was more of magic than science in its construction. This notion was reinforced somewhat when the small box itself began to make sounds in the strange tongue. Though the performance was impressive, the priests did not see that there was a great deal of value in a man being able to hold converse with a machine. Indeed one of the priests held that the contrivance was simply a kind of magical or mechanical parrot which the visitor was trying to train to repeat the words he spoke to it. Presently, the priests lost interest and went about their own tasks.

The exchange of information between Rudlan Others and Streven Luse lasted for two orbits of the ship. During each orbit, communication could only be maintained for about fifteen minutes, partly because of the range limitation of Rudlan's equipment and partly because of the intense interference by electrical storms that were almost a permanent phenomenon somewhere or other in the vast Antarctic rain forests.

Rudlan gave an account of the way in which the Martians had been received and treated in Noi Lantis. He also described as well as he could the size and appearance of the city, and made a rough estimate of the number of people living in it. Though the Martians had seen more of the palace and the temple than of the city itself, on their journey through its narrow streets they had observed enough to indicate that it was circular and about five kilometres in diameter, containing possibly between eight thousand and fifteen thousand people. Streven Luse asked about the scientific and cultural level of Noi Lantis; and having been shown the Temple of Godfred and its laboratories Rudlan could confidently report that the science was rudimentary, as Mirlena had originally suggested, and the equipment almost medieval.

As he listened to Rudlan's report in the Communications Room, while several other members of the expedition also heard the account from extension speakers, Captain Luse felt at least a sort of interim sense of relief. So far, the four people he had committed to the task of investigating Noi Lantis did not appear to be enduring any more serious hazard than the triple G stress of Earth. He was surprised as well as relieved to learn of the courtesy with which they were being treated. He wondered what Kord Vengel would make of it all. No doubt the Political Officer would turn in a lengthy and thoroughly depressing report at the first opportunity.

Meanwhile, since all was well so far with the Noi Lantis venture, the other investigation programme—which had been hastily revised to accommodate this unforeseeable project—could be continued. Most of the useful transmitting time on the first orbit had been taken up with the reports from ground. On the second orbit, Captain Luse informed Rudlan Others of the general content of some curiously conflicting messages he had been receiving. There now appeared to be an element of conflict at Marsbase. Senior members of the Political Division were taking a gloomy view of the investigation of Noi Lantis, and were strongly urging Streven Luse to recall the small team he had set down. On the other hand, the Scientific Divisions and the Administration were becoming more enthusiastic about the project; and there had even been suggestions that Captain Luse should try to find some way of extending the total amount of time allowed for the venture.

With all the other scientific work that had to be done, Streven Luse was in no mood for getting involved with conflicts of opinion on Mars. In reply to the many and frequently wordy texts from Marsbase, he had sent a volley of moderately evasive replies, all of which really boiled down to, "Your message received and understood." The Captain felt that, one way or another, he had had quite enough interference with the original expedition programme. He was not now prepared to tolerate interference with interference. He told Rudlan drily that the whole conflict had clearly been triggered by the cypher messages transmitted back to Mars by Dr. Stroza and Kord Vengel, and remarked that he was exceptionally glad they were not in a position to add fuel to the flames.

He also told Rudlan Others that he was going to use the sloop to set down another four-man investigation team on Earth. This time it would be for a purely physical investigation under the leadership of Meiron Menders. The touch-down area had been carefully selected for its geophysical and historical interest. It was near to the remains of the ancient city of Brasilia, one capital of the United States of South America. Brasilia had been chosen because it was on a plateau more than a thousand metres above the sea-level that had existed before the disintegration of Luna. It had also been built about two thousand kilometres from the ocean; and, therefore, it would probably offer more interesting remains than many of the world's other major cities, which had existed either on low ground or near the sea and had first been inundated, then swept away by the receding waters. When

Meiron Menders and his team had been set down together with their equipment, the sloop would probably be recalled to orbit for its eventual rendezvous with the Noi Lantis team.

After these exchanges of information had been made, the exploratory vessel was again approaching the radio horizon. Rudlan Others did not think it would be worth keeping watch for another orbit, so he called that he would close down and make contact again on the following day.

Captain Luse had the last and ominous word. "So all I have to worry about now," he said without humour, "is that things seem to be going too well. Next contact in about thirty hours, Rudlan. Out."

. . .

Mirlena returned from her interview with Urlanrey feeling quite as exhausted as she had told Kord Vengel she had been when he had pressed her to go on the tour of Noi Lantis. She was escorted back to her chamber in the King's Retreat by the officer of the Pryterguard who had taken her to the palace.

When she was alone, she lay gratefully on her bed and let out a sigh of relief. It was not that the discussion with Urlanrey had tired her, she reflected with bitter amusement, but that a combination of Earth gravity and some rather strenuous lovemaking was just about as much as any superbly fit female negro psychologist from Mars could be expected to bear.

She tried to analyse her relationship with Kymri, but was too confused to make any sense out of it. Could it simply be a manifestation of that ancient and perverse sexual impulse to self-degradation—the impulse that, throughout history, had compelled certain types of men to ruin themselves for the sake of women and certain types of women to take pleasure in humiliation for the sake of love? Or was it possible that she, an educated woman of an advanced society, could establish some valid bond with a half-civilized white man belonging to a dying culture? Or was she simply experimenting with new forms of sexual excitement—a strange, bitter-sweet titillation of the senses? She did not know. Possibly she would never know. She was aware only that she had achieved greater involvement in those two clandestine encounters with Kymri than with any other man she had known.

Tired, and not a little depressed by this useless attempt at introspection, she fell asleep—and slept through the rest of the morning and most of the afternoon. Rudlan Others came once or twice to see that she was all right; but he did not disturb her. He was a sensitive man; and he had a great affection for Mirlena. Already he was beginning to suspect that her relationship with Kymri was more complex than it seemed.

She slept long and deeply—until she was literally shaken back into consciousness by an anxious and unhappy Garl Sinjorge.

"Mirlena! Wake up! For Vaney's sake, wake up. It's Kord Vengel—he's disappeared!"

CHAPTER TWENTY-SEVEN

Kymriso, Second Consul and most powerful woman in Noi Lantis, sat on the couch in her apartment in the Dragon Palace, and regarded her son with affection and exasperation. She was, she knew, very beautiful. Kymri was both proud of her beauty and jealous of it—looking angrily or suspiciously at every man who admired her. Every man except two: Stasius and Urlanrey. But the estrangement that existed between Kymriso and her son was not because many men, including the king and the Lord of the Generators, were interested in his mother. It was because she had never told him the name of his father. He felt that, even though there might be good reasons for the knowledge remaining secret from others, Kymriso could at least have trusted her own son thus far.

Kymri had accepted the wine that she had offered him, but declined to sit on the couch beside her. Instead, he sat cross-legged on a skin rug, looking up at her, admiring as always the long red-gold hair and the complexion that might have belonged to a young girl.

"I had hoped that you might visit me earlier," she said softly. "I did not care to have to send a messenger. Is there, then, so little affection between us?"

Sometimes, when he was with her, Kymri felt awkward and tongue-tied. This was one of those times. It was not made easier by the fact that she wore a black tunic trimmed with gold thread—he had never seen Kymriso wear black before—and he was somehow incongruously reminded of Mirlena.

"Madam—mother—I mean, Kymriso," he stammered, suddenly recalling that she hated him to use the word mother, "the king commanded me to attend upon the visitors. Otherwise, I would have come to you as soon as I had returned to Noi Lantis."

She smiled faintly. "So much for a young man's harmless elsdykik. You went into the forest to seek guidance from Godfred, to discover if you should press your application for the priesthood, despite my disapproval. You return not with the guidance of Godfred but with a problem that may well rock the foundations of Noi Lantis. The king is not pleased."

"It was not my desire to—"

"Hold!" said Kymriso. The message box that was fitted in the homes of all people judged sufficiently important to enjoy the privilege was clicking away. Kymriso rose from the couch, went to the small machine and pressed the silver stud that indicated she was ready to receive the message. She listened intently, her eyes seeming to focus on nothing at all, while the needle jerked busily in response to electromagnetic impulses, making its mysterious pattern of clicks.

Kymriso was one of the very few women in Noi Lantis—all of them being high-born—who had been instructed in the secret language of wire messages. Kymri envied her the knowledge. He would have given much to be able to share it.

There was no expression on her beautiful face as she received the message, but her lips moved perceptibly, silently forming the words as she interpreted them from the uneven series of clicks. Kymri waited patiently till the message had ended—it was not long, and there was no way of determining from her reaction whether it was important or trivial—then he gave Kymriso a look of enquiry.

"It is of little consequence—for the moment," she said enigmatically. "The most important thing, concerning us all, is what we are to do about these black visitors you have brought."

"There is little to be done," said Kymri hesitantly. "The king, with wisdom, treats them as honoured guests . . . Presently, they will depart, and that will be the end of it."

"Will it?" Kymriso treated her son to a penetrating gaze. "Or will it be the beginning of something that spells disaster for Noi Lantis?"

He looked at her miserably. "I do not know."

"These people are powerful and dangerous," went on Kymriso. "If I understand correctly, their race is numbered in many, many thousands. It will be strange indeed if they do not return with others of their kind, offering not the hand of friendship but the whip of mastery . . . Is that not so?

"The girl Yosseline, who was my robing woman," said Kymriso with sudden, apparent irrelevance. "Have you spoken with her since your return?"

Kymri was surprised. "I have not even thought of her."

Kymriso smiled. "Strange. Strange indeed. There was a time when you thought of little else." She poured herself some wine. Then she said calmly: "Is it so much more wonderful to be between the legs of a black woman who speaks a strange language, wears male garments, commands in the presence of men, and whose womb—for all you know—may carry the seed of monsters?"

Kymri dropped his glass of wine, and looked at his mother, appalled. "How do you know this thing?"

Kymriso gave a bitter laugh. "The Hall of the King's Retreat contains many secrets . . . If it is prudent to attend to the needs of strange and powerful guests, is it not wise also to observe their actions?"

Kymri wanted to weep with shame and humiliation. He wanted to kill himself and Mirlena. Above all he wanted to escape from the presence of this beautiful woman whom he had worshipped as a child and whom he had learned to fear as a man.

But he could not move. The power of decision seemed to have gone from his mind and the power of action from his body.

"It seems, Kymri," she went on with surprising gentleness, "that Godfred amuses himself vastly with us all . . . Do you love this—this woman you call Mirlena?"

"Tell me what love is," he managed to say, "and I will answer you."

She held out her hand to him. As he took it, wonderingly, Kymri sensed a sadness and loneliness in the woman who seemed always to surprise him with every word she spoke.

"There is not time enough. Nor is it fitting. But I will tell you something of much greater moment, so that you may weigh such matters as love and loyalty and duty in the light of knowledge . . . what do you think will happen when Urlanrey dies?"

"Stasius and the consuls, of whom you are one, will elect a new king."

"They will not."

"But the king's wife gave him only girl children."

"True," agreed Kymriso. "But the king's mistress gave him a son . . . You know that I have lain with Urlanrey, you know that I have lain with Stasius." She sighed. "Where does ambition end and desire begin? You have never known me, Kymri. Perhaps I have never really known myself. I had too strong a mind and too passionate a body for marriage; though perhaps there have been one or two high-born men who would have granted me more freedom in marriage than they would have given any other woman . . . Be that as it may, rejecting marriage, how else could I achieve the position and power I desired? My first conquest was a priest of electrics, my second was the palace comptroller, my third was a consul who died before you were born, my fourth was Stasius, and then Urlanrey. I lied to none, I cheated none. Therein lay my strength.

"Do not forgive me, Kymri. I have no need of forgiveness. I am content . . . But now that you have seen fit to consort with those who endanger Noi Lantis, you must continue the game knowing that you are more than a young man bent on folly."

Kymri's mind was reeling. "Why could you not tell me before?" he asked desperately. "Was it because Urlanrey would not recognize me." He gave a bitter laugh. "The Pryterguard could have removed the problem without difficulty."

"Child! Child! Urlanrey has much affection for you. That is why he required secrecy, why he showed no sign of favour. Think what would have happened if it had been common knowledge that you were the king's only and illegitimate son. A party would have formed about you, seeking to establish your legitimate claim to the dragon throne. Ambitious men would have seen your cause as a possibility for their own advancement, urging that age abdicate in favour of youth. Such a movement might rapidly have brought the shedding of blood, as has been known before in our history. And be sure that the blood spilled would have been yours, not Urlanrey's. He is not one of the great kings of Noi Lantis; but he is one of the careful ones, one of the wise ones. He knows that we are not such a large nation that we can be enemies to each other. He knows that the forest is our true enemy, and now . . . And now, also, these strangers from Mars . . . The king has acknowledged your claim under his own seal. It will be published at his death."

Kymri did not know what to say. As always, Kymriso, beautiful and intelligent, had reduced him to incoherence.

"Does the king know that I know?" he managed at last.

"He knows of certain matters between you and the Lady Mirlena. He thought the time had come for you to be aware of your destiny . . . You have a high duty; and desire is, after all, a double blade."

Kymri was still mystified. "What do you mean by that?"

Kymriso laughed. "It amuses Godfred to choose me, of all people, to tell you not to be weak for a woman but to use a woman's weakness for your own purposes, which must be the good of your own race."

"I have never forgotten my duty to Noi Lantis and the king."

Kymriso shrugged. "If matters we have spoken of were known, some might dispute that . . . Today, in the company of Stasius, you escorted two of the black strangers through our city. When did you last see these two?"

"When I took them back to their chambers in the King's Retreat. They needed to rest, being more accustomed to their own world where, it seems, all things are less heavy."

"The wire message that I received when we were talking—it informed me that one of the two has disappeared. A search has been carried out, but the man cannot be found."

"A man cannot disappear for long," said Kymri, "unless he takes to the forest."

Kymriso shrugged. "Who knows what is or is not possible for these black ones from Mars. Embrace me, Kymri, and let us be friends. Then follow your duty wherever it may lead."

CHAPTER TWENTY-EIGHT

The light was beginning to fade. As he hurried back to the Hall of the King's Retreat, Kymri glanced at one of the many temple clepsydras—a beautiful machine of glass bulbs, tubes, copper spindles and pointers, powered by green-shaded water—and saw that it was nearly the twentieth hour. Soon, the Lord of the Generators would command the lighting of the lamps.

Kymri found the three remaining Martians deep in discussion in the chamber shared by Garl Sinjorge and Kord Vengel. They were talking in their own language; and though he was able to understand snatches of what they were saying, Kymri realized that they were talking too fast for him to make much sense out of the few words he recognized.

Mirlena smiled at him, but Garl and Rudlan, having briefly noted his presence, ignored him. He waited patiently for Mirlena to speak to him in his own language.

Presently, there was a subdued and distant hum, and the carbon-filament lamps came dully to life. Mirlena made a sign to her companions, who continued their discussion in lowered voices, and came towards Kymri. He was standing by the yellow-paned window, watching the eerie amber glow of the electrics at the Dragon Palace, less than a kaymet away.

"You know that we cannot find Kord Vengel."

"Yes. A wire message brought the news to my mother, when I was visiting her."

"Your mother is a very important woman," observed Mirlena. "Also very beautiful."

He smiled. "Even by your standards?"

"By any standards . . . Kymri, I have no right to ask you this, but I believe you and I can trust each other a little. Do you think there is any reason why Urlanrey—or any of your people—should want to keep Kord a prisoner?"

He looked shocked. "He is the king's guest."

"You were once our guest," she reminded him, "yet a prisoner also."

"That was different. We fought and—and you overcame me." He smiled grimly. "The savage had to be taught that he could not defeat civilized people with their fearful weapons . . ."

"The king might believe that a valuable hostage would guarantee our good conduct and that of our companions in the sky ship."

Kymri shook his head. "Urlanrey is not foolish. Neither will he act dishonourably to acknowledged guests."

"That was my thought also," said Mirlena. "Rudlan mentioned the possibility, but I do not think he took it seriously . . . Garl has suggested the most probable explanation, but I have not mentioned it to the Pryterguard or any of the priests who are now looking for Kord . . . I thought I would talk to you first."

"What is this possible explanation, then?"

"Garl thinks that Kord has gone into the tower you call the Abode of the Dead."

Kymri was incredulous. "But was not Kord Vengel warned that this is holy ground? Was he not told by Stasius that few are privileged to pass through its doorway? Also, was it not made known to him that the penalty for desecration is death?"

Mirlena laughed harshly. "I see, Kymri, that you do not understand Kord Vengel. To him, you of Noi Lantis are primitive white savages. He does not respect your traditions or beliefs.

He thinks that we negroes are the superior race, and that whatever we do to you white people can be justified because of what happened two thousand years ago."

"You are wrong. I know Kord Vengel . . . But if he has visited the Abode of the Dead, and if he does not return, there the matter may rest."

"No, even if he does not come back, the matter cannot rest. We have to be able to explain to our own people on Mars what has happened to him. He is an important man, Kymri. If my government suspects—as they would, in the absence of facts—that you people of Noi Lantis are responsible for his disappearance, there is no telling what may happen."

"I see . . . Why does Garl Sinjorge believe that this man has entered the Abode of the Dead?"

"Because last night, while you and I were engaged in other things, Kord spoke a great deal and with much excitement of the tower. It is the only tower in Noi Lantis that is not made of stone blocks. It is made of a substance we call concrete."

"What is concrete?"

"Exactly. You do not know. And that is why Kord was excited. After you brought him back from the tour of the city today, he spent much time looking at the Abode of the Dead through his field glasses—the lenses through which distant things seem near. He was also taking notes of the movements of the priests; and he told Garl that for two minutes in every hour no one could observe if the tower was being entered. He also told Garl that the top of the tower was an observatory, and that it appeared to contain a telescope and tracking instruments—that is, machines that are able to watch far movements in the skies. Now do you understand why the tower fascinated him?"

Kymri was silent for a while. Then he said: "The penalty for entering the tower is death. Not even the Pryterguard may go into the Abode of the Dead."

"This we know," said Mirlena wearily. "Whatever happens now, there is bound to be some terrible disaster . . . I had hoped for so much from this visit to Noi Lantis. I had hoped so much that white people and black people might look upon each other—as you and I have done—to see what is good, not what is evil . . . But now this fool, this stupid bigoted idiot of a man, is jeopardizing the destinies of two worlds because he thinks that a black skin entitles him to do whatever he wishes."

There were tears in her eyes. Suddenly, Mirlena felt very tired. Not tired because of Earth gravity. Tired in the depths of her spirit. Tired because an impossible dream was about to be proved impossible.

Suddenly and crazily, Kymri was light-hearted. Suddenly, Godfred had filled him with the death-wish once more, as when he had given battle to the sky beast. Suddenly, there was fire in his veins and steel in his heart.

"Kymriso, my mother, spoke to me of many things," he said softly, "but her last command was that I should follow my duty wherever it may lead. It amuses Godfred, the divine joker, to lead me to the Abode of the Dead. It amuses Godfred to spur me to seek and save one whom I despise . . . It amuses Godfred also to appoint you, Mirlena, to accompany me in this dreadful act. Tell these, your friends, that presently we shall go to seek their comrade. Tell them also that you and I have looked upon each other, have touched each other, have loved each other and are not ashamed."

Mirlena looked at him wide-eyed. There was too much to say and nothing to say. Kymri had said only what she was afraid to think. The black Martian psychologist was annihilated. All that remained was a woman, knowing only that the colour of woman is as the colour of man.

She was proud and terrified. She was unable to think; yet she perceived with a greater clarity than ever before in her life the thing that mattered.

She pulled herself together, and spoke rapidly and confidently to Rudlan Others and Garl Sinjorge.

When she had finished, Rudlan Others held out his hand to Kymri. The hand was shaking. It was the first time he had ever touched a white man.

Garl Sinjorge could not bring himself to hold out his hand; and was bitterly ashamed.

CHAPTER TWENTY-NINE

Timon Harland, President of Mars, sat in his twentieth-storey private office in the Palace of the Republic, looking out through his window, across the roof-tops of the capital, across the far blue waters of Broken Lake towards the sharp, still uneroded peaks of the Red Range. He was trying, without a great deal of success, to think about nothing at all. He was trying to think about nothing at all because he was probably going to have to kill a man.

Timon Harland was old and dispirited. He had been in office too long; but, being Kastril's man, he had to stay in office. Gondomar Kastril, First Secretary of the Vaney Party, needed a symbol—a symbol of progress and humanism. Timon Harland was that symbol.

It was strange, reflected the President, how once upon a time —many years ago, too many years ago—he and Gondomar had been young idealists dedicated in friendship and a common purpose. Temperamentally, Timon Harland was the thinker, the theorist: temperamentally, Gondomar Kastril was the man of action. When they were young, Kastril had been content to leave all the thinking, all the theorizing and long-range philosophizing to his friend. Kastril's one aim was to achieve enough political power to put Harland's humanism and brave ideas into practice. Among their acquaintances, they had been known as the Yogi and the Commissar, after the characters in a middle-period musical drama.

But that was a long time ago. Now, not even the most powerful trivee commentators or Independent Seaters (there were only seven left in Congress) could make any light reference to the President or the First Secretary. It was too dangerous.

Over the years Kastril had hardened, and Harland had softened. As he achieved political power, Kastril found that he did not need ideas and new theories: power was satisfying in itself. What he did need, however, was the reputation for integrity that Timon Harland had acquired without seeking or wanting it, while Kastril was acquiring the power he both sought and wanted for its own sake.

So the unworldly Harland had become the front man, the figurehead, while Kastril and the butchers of his Political Office maintained absolute power by the ancient means of terror and liquidation. All this Timon Harland saw clearly in retrospect. It was a great pity that he had not been able to see it in prospect. So much misery might have been saved: so many good lives might not have been lost.

The trouble with Timon Harland was that in younger years, he had thought too much and too abstractedly, and had felt too little. He had also been naïve. He had accepted everyone and everything on their face value. He saw no reason for not believing everything that Kastril told him; and if Kastril announced—with convincing personal sadness—that friends had suddenly become traitors, seeking to destroy the achievement and stability of the State, Harland would simply grieve at a personal loss, grieve that he would see familiar faces no more.

If Harland had been naïve to the point of lunacy, Kastril had been cunning to the point of genius. He kept his figurehead in isolation. At first it was discreet, so that for many years the

President was unaware that old comrades were not allowed t
see him. If he gave a party and invited someone of whom Kastr
did not approve, that someone either declined the invitation an
had an illness or accepted the invitation and had an accident.
Harland tried to call someone who was politically undesirable
the line was out of order, or his whereabouts were unknown or –
and this, too, had happened a lot—he was eventually allowed t
talk to the President with a needle gun at his head just to ensur
that he said the right things.

Constitutionally, any congressman—including Independen
Seaters—had the right of private access to the President o
matters of planetary emergency. Two Independent Seaters ha
exercised their privilege and had tried to warn Harland—in th
days when he still believed in Kastril—what the First Secretar
was doing. They had died. Not immediately afterwards. But the
had died within a week or two and quite accidentally. The mess
age was clear to everyone except the President.

For a long time, President Harland believed that the Compan
of Secret Police assigned to him had been assigned to him for hi
own welfare, to protect him against maniacs, cranks, busybodies
undesirables and the innumerable little people who felt they ha
a personal right to pester their President. But now he knew that
in reality, the Secret Police were his jailers. They watched ever
move, screened or terrorized every contact, planned and fixe
every public appearance. They were Gondomar Kastril's élite
entrusted with the surveillance and almost the complete contro
of movement of the only free political prisoner in the Republi
of Mars.

Timon Harland had never been interested in women and ha
never married. Which was unfortunate. Because in a bedroom, in
the intimacy of a shared life, a woman might have whispered
something that would have awakened him to the true state of
affairs. But President Harland did eventually discover the truth
in his bedroom—the hard way—by holding a dying man in his
arms for three or four minutes while seven other men paid with
their lives to buy that precious time.

When Kastril's élite finally shot their way into the room, they found a dead man sprawled on the floor and the President in a state of shock. He still had the wit to say that the man had been too wounded to do or say anything. But when Kastril himself arrived and looked at the President, each of them knew.

After the 'attempted assassination' Kastril doubled the presidential Security Force. It was then that President Harland came to the bitter conclusion that it was his duty as a Martian to destroy Gondomar Kastril, who had been his friend and was now First Secretary of the Vaney Party.

He could not destroy him politically—Gondomar was too strong. So Harland would have to destroy him physically—a loathsome thought. The President, hyper-sensitive and an intellectual, had always held himself aloof from matters physical. They terrified him. Perhaps that was partly why he had been so gullible for so long. Perhaps that was why he was not fit to be President of Mars.

Taped under the bottom of the third drawer in the President's desk there was a miniature needle gun. It had taken considerable time and ingenuity for Timon Harland to smuggle it into his office. Each time he passed the guards in the outer chamber, he was scanned electronically—in case, so Kastril had assured him, anyone succeeded in planting some kind of dangerous device in his clothes or possessions. But by then Harland was wise enough to know that the scanning was in case he carried any weapon of his own that the Security Force did not know about. Gondomar Kastril was one of the few men ever admitted to the President's private office. The First Secretary always carried his own needle gun; but then he was the First Secretary. It had occurred to the President that if Kastril ever wanted him to 'commit suicide', the private office was probably where it would be arranged.

The President had noticed that the electronic scanner did not seem to scan below the bottom of his trousers. Therefore Harland had begun to come to the Palace of the Republic in his largest shoes, with components of the miniature needle gun hidden in the toe-caps. It had taken him no more than half a dozen visits, and had cost him no more than a few bruised toes, to get all the parts into his office.

Now the weapon was reassembled. It merely remained for him to discover if he had the nerve to use it.

The President glanced at his desk clock. The First Secretary was due in a few more minutes. Carefully, Harland half pulled out the fourth drawer, felt under the bottom of the third and removed his only and ultimate instrument of policy. He slipped it into his pocket. It was so compact that the slight bulge would not be noticed.

Then he began to gaze through the window again, his eyes in nearer focus. This time his attention was caught by the huge Vaney Column that dominated the Capital.

Long ago, Timon Harland had done a considerable amount of research on Thomas Vaney. Enough to know that he never had any positive political philosophy, apart from seeking equal rights and equal opportunities for others of his race. Enough to know that his real name was Thomas Mulvaney and that his great-grandfather had emigrated to America from a small European country called Ireland. Enough to know that Mulvaney, the rabble-rouser, was ill-educated and not very intelligent; that his only real assets were his magnificent voice and appearance; that his speeches had been written for him by a group of militant negroes known as the Power Men; and that it was the Power Men who had exploited Mulvaney's death—and had probably even assassinated him—in order to carry their war with the white man to the very depths of space.

But in the course of two thousand years, history had been re-written many times. The early-period histories recorded that Vaney, the pure negro, had been shot; the middle-period histories were beginning to claim that he had been nailed to a wooden cross by a group of maniacal white men oddly called the Klux.

As he looked at the gigantic figure poised on top of Vaney Column in a noble attitude of pride and defiance, Harland smiled grimly to himself. Such was the evolution of truth.

The President became aware of a short, interrupted low-rhythm buzz. He took the pebble receiver from his pocket and pressed a tiny, jewelled stud.

"Mr. President, the First Secretary has arrived at the Palace.

He will be with you in a few moments."

Harland recognized the voice of Oran Maig, his personal assistant. She was a good, loyal girl. But recently, she seemed to be getting rather friendly with one of the new guards supplied by Kastril—what was his name? Stovro. Lieutenant Stovro. The President sighed. Oran was one of the two or three people he could talk to. Or, at least, she had been. Now he was not so sure.

"Thank you, Oran. I am ready to receive him."

But was he ready? Timon Harland did not know. Soon he would find out.

"Timon, my old friend. How are you? How are you?" As usual, the First Secretary burst into the room like a whirlwind.

"Old," said the President evenly. "Too old. We both are."

"Nonsense! Nonsense! Our bodies may not be quite so strong as they were," Kastril thumped his corpulent stomach with some complacency, "but our hearts are still strong. That is what counts."

The President smiled. It was impossible not to admire the sheer animal vitality of the man. Kastril was like one of those odd little balls some scientist had been telling him about. They bounced higher and higher and went colder and colder as they bounced.

"Do you remember when we were both young, Gondo?" he said.

The First Secretary looked at him in surprise. "It is a long time since you called me Gondo. These days it is usually Mr. Secretary. I was beginning to think you had learned to dislike me."

"No, I don't dislike you. It would be easier if I did. I only fear you."

"Vaney! That's a thing to say to an old comrade . . . What is on your mind, Timon? In this room—the highest security room in the Palace, soundproofed and no bugs—you can say what you like."

"Do you remember when we were young, Gondo?" went on the President. "We used to sit talking through half the night, planning how we were going to build the great society on Mars."

Kastril laughed. "I remember. Two young world-changers . . . Only you did the talking and the planning, Timon. I just did the listening."

"Yes," agreed Harland. "You did the listening. That should have been my first warning . . . But they were good times, though. The years of promise."

Kastril sat down on his usual chair and yawned contentedly. "And now we have the years of fulfilment . . . You are in a black mood, Timon. Get out of it. Let us do each other a favour and take a couple of days off. They say there is some good deer hunting to be had in the South Alps."

"Ah, yes." The President looked as if he had not heard. "The great society . . . If we ever had enough power . . . Well, we got absolute power—or you did. But no great society. Only a community of fear."

"Timon, you *are* ill—or something. What the Vaney is it? Out with it, man." Again Kastril laughed, but his eyes were cold and suspicious. "There's nothing that can't be settled between friends."

"What are you going to do about Earth?"

"Ah, I thought it was that! " The First Secretary seemed almost relieved. "Only one thing to do, Timon. You must know that . . . My political man—what's his name?, Vargel or Vengel, something like that—says they are potentially dangerous. Not now, of course. But give them a century or two—especially if we set up Mars-Earth traffic. The risk is too great, Timon."

"The psychologist does not envisage any danger. She says—"

Kastril grinned. "Psychology is bunk, and women psychologists—oh, but I'm sorry, old comrade. I have just remembered she was nominated by the Presidential Commission. Still, I stand by what I say. Psychology is bunk. History is what counts . . . They say it repeats itself. But this is one piece of history that won't be repeated. For decency's sake I shall wait until we get the full reports; but I'm afraid in the end I shall have to sign the order."

"I'm sorry, Gondo," said the President taking the needle gun out of his pocket, "but you won't be signing anything any more.

154

The human race can't afford it."

"Timon, what the. Vaney!" Kastril made a move to his own gun.

"Don't," said the President softly. "Goodbye, Gondo. Perhaps we have both lived too long." He pressed the stud, and an unseen brilliantly white needle of energy leaped across the office and passed through Gondomar Kastril's brain.

For a moment or two, the President stood paralysed, looking down at the body of the man who had shielded him from all the dreadful facts of political life for so long. There was an almost comical look of surprise on Kastril's face—as if he still did not believe that the intellectual could play the man of action.

Harland himself began to share in that surprise; for suddenly his brain seemed brilliantly clear. There was a chance. There was still a chance to destroy the community of fear, a chance to aim once more for the great society. If he could stay alive.

He knelt by Kastril's body, took the still warm hand and pressed it on the stud of the First Secretary's needle gun. He aimed it as well as he could at his own shoulder, then looked away and pressed the stud. The pain was oddly not as great as he would have imagined. Which was fortunate because there was no time to faint.

When the fire had stopped dancing through his shoulder and neck, he struggled unsteadily to his feet. He got as far as the desk, and slumped in his chair for a while. Then, with a tremendous effort of will, he pulled himself together.

President Harland pressed the emergency all-stations switch on his desk transceiver.

He cleared his throat and spoke. "This is your President speaking. I have some bad news, but I ask you all to stay calm. First Secretary Kastril, who is now dead, has attempted to assassinate me. I am alive but wounded. I request all Secretary Kastril's Security Forces to lay down their arms and remain at their posts. They will come to no harm. I further request the immediate support and attendance of my own aides, assistants and the senior members of the Presidential Commission. I also request, in the name of the people of Mars, an immediate resumption of Congress to investigate the effects of First Secretary Kastril's Political and Security activities during his term of office. This is President Harland speaking. I ask you all to stay calm."

He switched off the transceiver, picked up his needle gun once more and waited grimly to see who would first come through the door. He bet himself that it would be one of Kastril's men with a sweep rifle.

He was right—and wrong.

Lieutenant Stovro and Oran Maig. Both armed. Just possibly he could kill one or both. But he didn't want to kill any more. He had had enough of killing. He put down his gun.

Stovro glanced at the dead. First Secretary, then turned to the President. "Congratulations, sir!" With one hand he trained his sweep rifle on the doorway. With the other hand he was tearing off his Security insignia. "There are six or seven of *us* in the Palace, sir, but there are about forty of *them*. Some of them will do as you asked, but some will come shooting. Oran has already alerted the Freedom Corps. If we can hold till they get here, we shall be all right."

President Harland was old, tired, wounded, confused. He did not know why Stovro should tear off his Security epaulettes with such obvious pleasure; he did not know how Oran Maig could alert something called the Freedom Corps; he did not even know what the Freedom Corps was. But he did understand what the word freedom meant.

And his reading of history—Martian history and the history of Earth—had taught him that no tyranny that had ever existed had been able to eradicate the desire for freedom from men's minds. It had only been able to force them to conceal it.

The President was old and tired, and his shoulder now hurt abominably. As he slipped into unconsciousness, he heard running footsteps in the Palace corridors, the penetrating hiss of sweep rifles, the shouts and cries of men.

Later, when the doctors were dealing with him and the tearing pain had been numbed, he heard another sound.

He did not know what it was until they told him.

Then he did not believe them, so they opened the windows and let him hear for himself . . .

Singing in the streets . . .

CHAPTER THIRTY

It was late in the evening. Fortunately, as usual, the sky was heavily overcast; and a fine rain was falling. Kymri thought that the profound darkness would conceal his and Mirlena's entry into the Abode of the Dead. He was right.

He thought also that there was a chance that the terrible act of desecration might pass completely undetected—particularly if they were able to emerge from the tower again in darkness. He was wrong.

Previously, the Abode of the Dead had never been guarded. There had never been any need to guard it. The strangeness of its structure, its long-established holiness, the belief that it contained ghosts and the ferocious guardians of ghosts—these, together with the penalty for desecration, were sufficient to deter even the most curious citizen of Noi Lantis from attempting to satisfy his curiosity.

But, after the disappearance of Kord Vengel, Stasius had judged it wise to ask the king to have a guard placed on the entrance to the tower. He remembered the Martian's interest in the structure; and he thought it highly probable that, since Kord Vengel could not be found, he had defied tradition, tabu, law and the normal rules of hospitality to explore the only place in Noi Lantis that really interested him.

Stasius, astute and intelligent, had no illusions about this aggressive Martian visitor. He knew that the Political Officer despised the white people of Earth and that he would care nothing about offending them if he could do so and survive. Presently, if Kord Vengel could not be found elsewhere, Stasius would have to ask the king for permission to mount a search in the Abode of the Dead. He hoped that the Martian would be found elsewhere—alive or dead, it did not matter—for the tower contained mysteries that were not without danger and could only be apprehended dimly.

Meanwhile, two officers of the Pryterguard stood on duty at the steps leading to the doorway of the tower—just in case the remaining visitors decided to seek their companion themselves.

This Kymri did not know until, holding Mirlena's hand, he walked straight into one of the guards in the almost impenetrable darkness. Both men reacted quickly. Kymri was not faster, only luckier. His first blow found the guard's stomach, occasioning an agonized grunt. This enabled him to judge roughly where the man's head might be. He found it, but hurt himself on a light helmet. The blow, however, was sufficiently strong to drop the guard to his knees.

The remaining guard evidently heard the scuffle and stepped cautiously towards the noise. He bumped into Mirlena, knocking her over and falling over himself. Mirlena groaned softly. Kymri, groping wildly for her, found the second guard and hit out in fury. Then his hand touched a shoulder that was soft and feminine; and he helped Mirlena to her feet.

Intuitively, during the entire incident, they had not spoken to each other. As their feet cautiously explored the first step leading up to the doorway of the tower, Kymri and Mirlena heard further blows behind them. For a valuable moment or two the guards remained unaware that they were grappling with each other, which enabled Kymri and Mirlena to feel their way up the steps and enter the small portico that led to the tower door.

Kymri had seen the tower many times by daylight; but the interior of the portico was always in shadow, and he had never actually seen the door that gave entrance to the Abode of the Dead. Even if he had, he would not have known how to use it. It was a revolving door that would not revolve unless pressure—the approximate weight of a human being—were placed on one or both of the exposed segments of the circular metal plate at its base.

Mirlena felt the door in the darkness and realized what kind of entrance it was. She tried to move it with her hand, and was surprised that it did not swing freely. In the pocket of her trek suit, she carried a small electric torch; but she was reluctant to use it. The guards at the bottom of the steps had already picked themselves up and, realizing that they had been passed, were raising the alarm. Obviously, they did not care to approach the Abode of the Dead too closely themselves.

Mirlena let go of Kymri's hand. Experimentally, she stepped into the doorway. The pressure of her feet activated the mechanism; and with a faint hum the door revolved through one hundred and eighty degrees. She was inside the tower, but Kymri was still outside.

Mirlena stepped off the plate, took the torch from her pocket, and shone it upon herself, peering through the glass plates of the door into the outer darkness and beckoning. She could see nothing; but Kymri evidently understood what she wanted him to do. There was another brief humming, and then he stood beside her.

Through the glass of the door they could now see dancing flames that seemed to be converging on the tower. A number of priests or soldiers were obviously coming in response to the cries of the guards.

"Will they follow us?" asked Mirlena anxiously.

"I do not think so. Urlanrey alone can permit entry into the Abode of the Dead . . . But now they know that someone has dared to defy the king and those, if any, who occupy this place. It will not be long before Urlanrey discovers who has committed the crime." He laughed softly. "Truly, this is an elsdykik from which we shall derive little comfort. Thus one learns to appreciate the humour of Godfred . . . The door was interesting. I have not seen its like before, even in your vessel in the sky."

"If we are not to be followed," said Mirlena, "I can use my torch . . . Don't let go of my hand, Kymri. I think I am more afraid than you."

She shone the torch about them. The circular walls of the great tower were bare; but there was a wide circular shaft, constructed of metal girders, passing centrally through the floor and the high ceiling. To Kymri, it looked like a bottomless cage; but Mirlena knew what it was.

There would have to be an operating mechanism, unless it was remotely or photo-electrically controlled.

There was an operating mechanism. A simple press-button.

Mirlena put her fingers on it. Far below, in the bowels of the earth, there was a hum and an echoing bang.

Kymri's hand gripped Mirlena's more tightly, but she was glad of the pain.

Presently, the lift reached ground level, and the doors opened automatically. The cabin was softly lighted.

"Is it a trap?" asked Kymri.

"No. It is just a machine to take us on the next stage of the journey. Now we have to step into it, and then we can make it take us back where it came from."

Kymri smiled. "Let us hope also that in the end it will return us to the face of the earth."

When they stepped into the cabin, Mirlena studied the control panel. There were six small numbered squares, one of which, number five, was illuminated. Evidently, ground level was the fifth level. The sixth would doubtless be the observatory/tracking station at the top of the tower. She thought for a moment, then touched the fourth square, which immediately lit up. The doors closed, and the lift descended.

It did not seem to go down very far, perhaps ten or fifteen metres, as far as Mirlena could judge. The doors opened, and she and Kymri stepped out into a long well-lighted corridor.

It was clean and well-kept, looking almost as if it might be in daily use. The recessed lighting in the ceiling gave a faintly bluish light. The floor seemed to be made of some kind of grey plastic. The walls also were grey, a lighter shade; but the doors on each side of the corridor were in a variety of colours—possibly they were part of a colour-coding scheme. At the far end of the corridor, which was perhaps a hundred metres long, there was a large double door. It looked as if it could be made of glass.

"It seems that the dead sleep well," whispered Kymri. "None have yet risen to greet us."

"One thing is quite sure," said Mirlena. "The Abode of the Dead is not an abode of the dead. As you see, it cannot have been the work of the people of Noi Lantis, Kymri. The machinery and the materials are far beyond any of the science known to your priests . . . I think it may be some kind of refuge or scientific station built a long time ago. And yet everything is so clean and fresh, even the air . . . Well, let us try to solve the mystery . . . If Kord is down here, it shouldn't be too difficult to find him."

Mirlena stepped to the nearest door—a red one—and opened it. The room was very large and was packed with metal and plastic shelves on which were various cans, packages, metal, plastic and glass rods, coils of wire, tubes, and a large number of unidentifiable components that all seemed to have something to do with electricity. There were numbers and writing on the shelves. The writing looked a little like early period Martian; but Mirlena was unable to make sense of any of the words.

"Stores," said Mirlena, "mostly for electrics, I think . . . This is a chamber where such materials are kept until they are needed." She smiled thoughtfully. "I wondered how the temple priests got their copper wire. Perhaps Stasius comes down here for it."

"The Abode of the Dead is large, and we have little time," said Kymri. "Let us move quickly until we find what we seek—or until we ourselves are found."

The next room they entered had a blue door. It, too, was a store room, containing both electrical and mechanical equipment.

Then they tried a yellow door, and found that it led into a room evidently containing chemical and medical supplies. After that they tried a green door: the room was full of vacuum sealed jars, every one containing seeds.

Mirlena was beginning to be too excited to be afraid. Wild thoughts were shooting through her mind—thoughts that were fantastic, absurd, and quite possibly near to the truth.

They worked their way along the corridor, opening door after door. Every chamber seemed to be a store room of one kind or another. In one of the chambers, they found a grotesque collection of metal limbs, body segments, even heads. But these, as Mirlena realized, were not prosthetic parts for human beings but a store of parts for machines.

Mirlena knew very little about robots, but she knew enough to realize that the robotic equipment kept here was far in advance of any that was now being developed experimentally on Mars.

Kymri was utterly baffled by all that they had seen. Here was a strange and frightening and exciting world, hidden below the ordinary everyday world of Noi Lantis. The Abode of the Dead, as was well known, had existed for centuries. Its origin was lost in the mists of time, as was that of Noi Lantis. Could it be that the Abode of the Dead had even existed before Noi Lantis? His head hurt, and his thoughts were tumbling over themselves.

It was while they were in the robotic stores that they heard an echoing clang along the corridor. The lift was being used. Presently there was the sound of footsteps approaching. Heavy footsteps.

Mirlena had a small anagun and two optic bombs in her pocket. Kymri had no weapons at all. It had seemed pointless to bring a spear or a sword, when Mirlena possessed weapons that were many times more deadly.

"What shall we do?" she whispered.

"Stay still. What else is there to do? If it amuses Godfred to send trouble, it will find us. There is no need to meet it."

"You don't think it could be Kord?"

Kymri smiled. "Whatever else Kord Vengel may do, he does not shake the earth."

They crouched behind a row of robotic legs, and waited.

The door opened.

A robot, head and shoulders taller than either of them, entered the store chamber. It was a beautifully made machine—not massive and clumsy like the experimental Martian robots. It was humanoid in shape—though the bright metal head bore no resemblance to a human head—and its body even had a strange kind of grace.

The robot paused in the doorway and surveyed the store chamber. Mirlena and Kymri thought that they were well hidden behind the row of legs. But they were not.

The robot came straight towards them and stood still. Then it spoke. Neither Kymri nor Mirlena, their minds numbed by the encounter, could understand any of the words.

The robot waited a few moments. Mirlena, realizing that her anagun would be useless—how could one paralyse a steel body? —wondered dimly if the optic bomb would temporarily blind it. Kymri, with belated practicality, was preparing to hurl himself at the machine's legs, hoping to knock it over.

But suddenly, the robot turned away, ignoring them both. It went to one of the reinforced shelves and hoisted a chest segment in its arms. Then it left the chamber and retreated down the corridor.

Mirlena's knees gave way, and she crumpled in a heap. Kymri stroked her forehead and hair, murmuring meaningless but soothing words. Presently they were both sufficiently recovered to continue their exploration.

Each coloured door they opened revealed yet another kind of store room; and each coloured door they closed behind them brought them nearer to the double doors at the end of the corridor.

"Shall we try this one?" asked Mirlena. "Or shall we try one of the other levels?"

"We have seen many strange things thus far," said Kymri, "not the least of which was the man-machine. Let us see what Godfred has prepared for us in this final chamber."

Hand in hand, they went to the double doors.

Kymri pushed, but neither of the doors would open. There were no handles; and although the doors were made of glass, the glass was opaque.

Suddenly, a voice said in a language that was not quite the same as Kymri's language and not quite the same as early period Martian, but close enough to both to be comprehensible. "Are you human?"

They were both too shaken to respond for a moment or two. Then Mirlena said: "Yes, we are human."

"Please prepare to be scanned."

There was a click. Two small panels, one on each side of the doorway, slid to one side to reveal small lenses. Slowly and deliberately, the lenses inspected Kymri and Mirlena from head to toe.

Then the doors opened.

Beyond there was a short narrow passage with one door on each side and one at the end.

"Please go to the door at the end of the passage. You may inspect the other rooms later if you wish."

Silently, Kymri and Mirlena advanced. The door opened for them and they walked into a room that might once have been a combined office/living room. To Kymri it looked very strange indeed. To Mirlena it did not seem vastly different from her quarters on the space ship.

The room was well lighted, but the lighting was not visible. Apart from some rather spartan domestic furniture, there was a large desk and behind it a chair. Bones were heaped across the chair and the desk. A human skeleton.

Suddenly, the room darkened and what seemed to be a cube of white light formed about the desk.

All the colours of white diffused then coalesced.

The impossible happened. An apparently solid living man sat at the desk.

A negro.

He seemed to see Kymri and Mirlena in the darkness. He seemed to be smiling at them.

"Greetings," he said. "As I speak, I am the last living member of my race on Earth. As you in the future hear these words—if, indeed, they are to be heard by anyone—I shall probably have been dead for several centuries. The date on which I am making this recording is the tenth of June in the year two thousand one hundred and ninety-three. It is the date on which I have decided to die.

"Why do I wish to talk to you of the future when it seems improbable that the human race has any future? I do not know. Perhaps I am only talking to myself for my own bitter amusement. Or perhaps I simply refuse to believe that, after a million years of evolution, after ten thousand years of civilization and five centuries of magnificent scientific achievement, the human race can perish so easily. We developed terrible weapons, of course—a foolish thing to do. But the weapons would have been harmless if we had not matched them with terrible hatred and terrible fear.

"I am a scientist, the son of a scientist, born in this underground prison we have come to call New Atlantis. My parents, who are dead, came here when the prison was not a prison or a refuge. At the end of the twentieth century it was built as the International Antarctica Research Station. It housed the scientists of many nations, united in their pursuit of knowledge, united against their common enemy—Antarctica itself, the wide white silence. In those days it did not take a man long to die if he ventured far on the surface without a friend.

"But because some men had black skins like mine, while others had white skins like those of my friends who still live in New Atlantis, the moon was destroyed, the Earth was devastated, Mars became the home of a few isolated black survivors, and the freezing waste of Antarctica began to reverse their own history, as if seeking a new beginning.

"I do not know if there can be a new beginning. There are eighty-four of us here in New Atlantis—apart from the service robots. Some of us are still scientists; and we were all the sons and daughters of scientists. One of my friends, a biologist, assures me that if we are very careful we have enough biological material to begin again. By biological material, he means human beings. But human beings are not subject to the normal rules of chance, mathematics or biology. Simply because they are human.

"Even if we find that the radiation hazards fall and we can venture to the surface once more, how shall we expand? Many of us, the children of scientists, have already rejected science, believing that it has brought about the destruction of mankind. With each successive generation, a little more learning will be lost until, in the end, those who survive—and they will have to adapt to a terrible environment in order to survive—will have returned like Antarctica itself to their own prehistory.

"Today I am going to kill myself. I am going to kill myself for three reasons. The first, the most reasonable, is that I have a disease that cannot be cured. Once it might have been. But we do not have enough skills here now to cover the entire field of medicine as it could be covered less than a century ago, when hundreds of thousands of doctors throughout the world specialized in such ailments as mine. Here we have two doctors, one good, one reasonably good. They do their best. But the disease prospers; and I, its host, do not care to face the constant increase in pain.

"That is my first reason. The second reason is because I am lonely. I am the last of the black skins. It was this insane war about colour that destroyed a great race with a breathtaking future. I did not take part in this war, but I feel its guilt rest upon me as it rests upon those of my white and brown and yellow-skinned friends who still survive. Most of us in New Atlantis are white. Genetically, if there is any survival, white should be dominant. There are no coloured pairs. Perhaps that is a good thing. But, still, it is an odd strange loneliness to be the last of my race. Even if I were not ill, I do not think I would care to endure it.

"The third reason is that my friends—my white and brown and yellow-skinned friends—love me. I am proud that white women have offered to bear my children, so that I may have some personal stake in the future and so that my race will not wholly die. I am proud also that no white man would resent this. I would like children; but the prospect frightens me. Would the dark

167

skins be drawn to the dark skins, in the end reproducing on a smaller scale what has already happened? The risk may be low, but I dare not take it. That is why I must kill myself before I succumb to the warm and terrible compassion of women.

"My friends know that I intend to kill myself. They are prepared to indulge my fanciful desire to record words that may never be heard. That is why they have given me this disused supervisor's room on the Stores Level. I have made my farewells, and I shall not be disturbed any more by my friends of New Atlantis. I have already programmed against intrusion by the robots who use this level.

"They are self-replicating robots. Our predecessors constructed them. We cannot. Sometimes, I think the robots will outlast the human beings. They, after all, are not subject to the ordinary laws of decay. They can use spare parts and cannibalize. They can make their own components. Perhaps that is the ultimate biological punishment. Perhaps man will be replaced by his metal slaves. Perhaps, in the end, the programming will fail and these words will be heard only by a machine that cannot comprehend what it is like to love, how cold it is to be lonely, and how it hurts to hope.

"And yet, to be without hope is almost to be without sanity. I prefer to feel the pain of hope. I am the last negro on Earth, and my name no longer matters. It could be Thomas Mulvaney, or Martin Luther King, or Uncle Tom. But I am a man and feel as other men. I am proud of all of us, of whatever colour, for what we have achieved. And I am ashamed of all of us, of whatever colour, for what we have done with our achievements.

"I cannot talk into the silence any more. I am too tired and too lonely. If any who come after should hear these words, let them reflect that this poor ravaged planet was once a teeming temple of life; and that it is more easy to destroy a temple than to build one.

"I am forty-seven years old, and I feel the weight of centuries. My last and greatest regret is that I have never heard and shall never hear a wild bird singing."

The man in the cube of light seemed to dissolve into mist.

Then all the different colours came together once more, and the cube was white and opaque. Then it disappeared.

For a moment, there was complete darkness. Then the normal room lighting was restored.

The bones at the desk were just dry bones. A thin and even layer of fine grey dust lay all over them, and all over everything.

Mirlena looked at Kymri, not trusting herself to say anything. The gap of centuries was great; but the sadness had leaped across it and was embedded too deep for tears.

CHAPTER THIRTY-ONE

Meiron Menders had used the lateral jets to push the sloop about a kilometre away from the parent vessel. He was all set to back-track in orbit and take the downward trajectory to Brasilia. Everything was programmed. There remained nearly four minutes to firing point.

The young physicist was restless. His companions—Jol Quhern and Tam Mbela, who had been on the first touch-down, and Rayne Markesh, who had not been on any touch-down—were already in their contour berths, waiting patiently. But Meiron was restless, and worried. He was not worried about the Brasilia trajectory. He was worried chiefly about Mirlena Stroza and her companions. But chiefly about Mirlena.

Reports from Noi Lantis had been sketchy so far. Tantalizing, exciting—but sketchy. No doubt the full story would be available in six more days, when the Noi Lantis party were due back in orbit. But the really worrying thing was that Rudlan Others had missed his last check-in. It was not like Rudlan. He was not the kind of person to be stopped by failure of equipment. Given sufficient time, Rudlan was the kind of person who could knock a transmitter together from anything that was metal and would bend.

So when he did not send at the appointed time, there was cause for concern. Still, Meiron consoled himself, the real time to worry would be if he did not send during the next favourable transmitting period. By that time Meiron and his companions would be jaunting about in the desolate but geophysically fascinating wastes of the great South American plateau. No doubt Streven would keep them informed.

On impulse, Meiron raised the manual periscope and took a last look at the vessel that had transported sixteen people from the now hospitable and civilized planet of Mars to the inhospitable wreckage of Earth. Once it had been the Green Planet, the most fertile and surely the most beautiful in the entire solar system.

As he looked back at the parent ship, apparently motionless against the blackness of space and the frozen fire of stars, Meiron Menders was struck by an absurd and breath-taking thought. The long programme of climatic engineering that had taken the ingenuity and energy of generations of Martians to complete had turned a world that was hostile to life into a world that brought forth and sustained an abundance of life. Might not the same kind of programme be applied to Earth? True, its magnetic field was down to zero, its axis had changed, and hard radiation still presented serious problems practically everywhere except in Antarctica. But might not this moribund world be made to flourish once more and give up its still immense natural wealth for the benefit of man?

The kind of people who could build a beautiful vessel that could cross millions of miles of space to scavenge a dead world could surely extend themselves further to restore that world to life. Particularly since men had still managed to survive on Earth. White men, true. Savages, true. But still men. Could not they be reclaimed along with their ruined planet?

His thoughts were cut short by Tam Mbela.

"Meiron, stop day-dreaming and fasten yourself down. You

have fifty seconds to do it, otherwise we shall all be covered by physicist jam when we touch down at Brasilia."

Meiron laughed and strapped himself down. Once more his thoughts turned to Mirlena, hoping that all was well.

Firing point came and went—gently. With an even acceleration the sloop ploughed back along the orbit, gaining speed, reducing orbital velocity, and becoming prey to the G force of Earth.

The manoeuvre was an easy one—or should have been an easy one. Everything was programmed automatically, including the reversal of attitude when the sloop fell out of orbit and before it approached the high tenuous reaches of Earth's atmosphere.

But the reversal of attitude manoeuvre did not take place. It did not take place because of the failure of two layers of insulation in both lines of the secondary relays that controlled the reversal jets.

When Kymri op Kymriso had been picked up anaesthetized where he had fallen and taken aboard the sloop, various tiny tropical insects had been clinging to his cloak of firebird feathers, having patiently climbed to explore as he lay unable to move. Kymri had been decontaminated as soon as he was aboard the sloop. Tam Mbela had gone over him thoroughly.

But one small insect—a mutation of a tiny beetle, once one of the 180,000 species in the order of coleoptera, though no one would ever know—had fallen from the cloak and scuttled to safety behind the control console. Unfortunately, it was a voracious insect and when hungry would eat almost anything of organic origin. Unfortunately, the outer insulation of the relays controlling the reversal jets was made of Martian flax. As time passed it ate its way patiently through the flax. Then it sampled the hydrocarbon-based plastic, and found that digestible, too.

As the reversal relays closed, there was a short-circuit which annihilated the insect that had caused the damage. There were no duplicate circuits on the sloop. Everything had been sacrificed to compactness and lightness.

The sloop fell out of orbit and gathered speed. When the reversal did not take place at its appointed second, everyone on board knew what was going to happen.

It was impossible to break the fall by using the main rocket. Soon the sloop would hit the outer layers of the atmosphere, and friction would turn it into a bright man-made meteor.

Meiron did a lightning calculation and worked out that he had about ninety seconds before the heat-shroud sealed off radio communication.

His companions were talking, shouting, crying; but with a tremendous effort he retained control of himself. He called Streven Luse.

"Listen, Streven. No time to answer me. You'll get it from the tapes anyway, even if you're not there. Reversal control doesn't function. This is the end of the sloop—and of us. Tell Mirlena— I thought of her . . . And tell Mars . . . Tell Mars to make Earth live."

Meiron Menders never knew whether the heat-shroud had allowed him to complete the message. He sank back exhausted, his head exploding with strange fantasies of green and pleasant lands as the refrigeration system failed to cope with the terrible heat building up outside.

The sloop became a meteor. The meteor plunged brightly towards Earth, streaking towards the dead city of Brasilia.

Presently, there was a new crater in the high, arid Brazilian plateau.

Presently, the vast silent desert of South America acquired a small new scar, a small, enduring monument.

CHAPTER THIRTY-TWO

Kord Vengel was dead, crushed under the half-severed body of a robot, lying among fragments of glass and the charred remains of a large picture of a nude white woman.

Kymri and Mirlena had found him on the second level of New Atlantis. They had been working their way systematically down the levels. Already drunk with wonder and emotionally exhausted by their experience in the last chamber of the first level, they had carried on with their search almost like sleep-walkers and almost but not quite—impervious to the wonderful discoveries they made at every turn.

Beneath the stores section they had found a series of extensive installations that meant nothing at all to Kymri but made Mirlena's over-excited mind numb with admiration. She, a space-traveller, was well equipped to appreciate the ingenuity, the compact beauty of the hydroponics units. The tanks contained no nutrient, and no plants grew, but the system was neat and efficient and could certainly have provided enough food for the eighty-four people who once depended on it. Linked to the hydroponics complex was the re-cycling unit, in turn linked to the air-conditioning and waste-disposal plant. Close also to the re-cycling unit were the kitchens and the small hospital. Neither the waste food nor the dead would have had far to travel.

As they explored, Kymri and Mirlena encountered several robots; but the machines took little or no notice of them. On two occasions robots approached and spoke in a strange tongue, as if asking questions. But when they received no answers they went about their business. It seemed that whoever had designed the robots had conditioned them to use only a specialized machine-language such as had been developed long ago for the precise instruction of computers. It seemed also that, lacking human direction, the robots were not equipped to take major decisions and merely contented themselves by maintaining the installations for which they were responsible. Perhaps, thought Mirlena fancifully, there was no robotic concept for death. Perhaps these self-replicating machines had been content to wait for centuries, maintaining and repairing the underground refuge, secure in the robotic conviction that one day their absent masters would return . . .

As they descended from the fourth to the third level, and then from the third to the second level, they found that each successive section was more extensive than the last. They had been able to explore the stores area quite quickly. It had taken them much longer to look through the hydroponics plant, the re-cycling unit, the air-conditioning and waste-disposal chambers, the hospital and kitchens.

When they arrived at the second level, it was obvious that this was the domestic and recreational section. There were single, double and triple-roomed living apartments. There was a chamber that was obviously a small school-room, with accommodation for perhaps ten children; but though the furniture and equipment looked clean and bright, it could not have been used for well over a thousand years. There was also a small swimming-pool—dry now—and a gymnasium, and a theatre or meeting hall.

And at the end of the second level, there was an art gallery.

Or perhaps the long-dead inhabitants of New Atlantis had re-garded it as something more—their link with a vanished civiliza-tion, their precious museum of things past, their treasure-house of the human spirit.

Kord Vengel had found the gallery. Perhaps, as Mirlena and Kymri had done, he had worked his way through all the levels. Perhaps he had even listened to that sad message from the last negro on Earth.

But certainly, he had found the gallery.

And then something inside him must have snapped. Kord Vengel, whatever else he might have been, was not a coward. No doubt he had been able to contain the tension and the fear created by his lonely journey of discovery. But perhaps the one thing he could not prepare himself for was this overwhelming legacy of beauty—white beauty, conceived and executed by the minds and skills of white artists from a lost white culture—which had confronted him in the gallery.

There were artists on Mars, but their work was puny com-pared with the timeless masterpieces preserved here. The master-pieces that Kord Vengel, with the sweep rifle he had borrowed from Garl, had not been able to wholly destroy.

As Mirlena and Kymri stared at the bizarre scene of destruc-tion, Mirlena tried to reconstruct what must have happened.

The pictures and their frames were contained in glass cases, no doubt vacuum-sealed. As Kord Vengel, amazed, horrified, perhaps even humiliated by this treasure of superb talent, had crazily set about its destruction, an alarm device must have been set off. That, perhaps, would have brought the robot. No doubt the machine would simply have attempted to restrain the human being; but by that time Kord would be in no mood for restraint. With the rifle, he had almost managed to cut the robot in two. Did it then fall and crush him intentionally or by accident? No one would ever know.

Kymri broke a long silence. "We need seek for your comrade no more, little one. Doubtless, he received the death wish; and the man-machine conveyed his reward to him with the greetings of Godfred . . . Now must we look to the preservation of our own lives, for I fear Urlanrey will display little joy over the matter of our recent actions." He gazed round at the charred and shattered pictures and at the few surviving ones with awe. "It is a pity that one man can destroy so much greatness. Do you think these pictures, which are such that I could wish to dwell upon their mysteries throughout the days of my life, are the work of those who once lived here below the face of the Earth? If so, they were truly great ones."

Mirlena, shaking the film of tears from her eyes, looked at the masterpieces that had been destroyed and at those that remained. She did not know who had painted them or to what period they belonged. She knew only that such artists had lived before the blessing and the curse of science had enabled man to assist in the destruction of his own planet.

"These paintings," she said, trying to keep her voice calm, "were made when Earth was full of cities and people. They are all that remains of a civilization that has gone."

She wished she could read the inscriptions on the frames; but even if she could, the titles of the pictures and the names of the artists would have meant nothing to her.

Except perhaps for one name. Even on Mars one artist-scientist of Earth, a giant of time, had been great enough for his name to endure in the history books.

But the long, brave survival of Leonardo da Vinci's master-piece had come to an end. The *Mona Lisa* had had her throat cut and her face blacked by Kord Vengel's sweep rifle.

The picture that lay in sorry remnants near his body had once been known to millions as *The Naked Maja* by the Spaniard, Goya. Among the other casualties to Martian fanaticism were *The Women Bathers* by Renoir, *Olympia* by Manet, *Danseuse à la Barre* by Dégas.

Even if she could translate the inscriptions on the frames, the names, the titles would mean nothing to Mirlena. But genius needs no name or title. Mirlena knew she was in the presence of works of genius.

But there was something odd. Something very odd. Mirlena did not know what it was until she compared the surviving pictures with the casualties. Among the survivors was the portrait of a jolly, long-haired white man—once known as *The Laughing Cavalier* by Franz Hals; a picture of a strange conveyance in an impossible and beautiful landscape—*The Hay Wain* by Constable; an enormous group of burning, almost living blossoms—*Sunflowers* by Van Gogh.

Mirlena looked at these survivors and several more. Then she turned again to the casualties. White women whose breasts, buttocks, bellies, arms, legs and faces had been disfigured by the energy of the sweep rifle.

She thought of Kord as she remembered him. Then she said softly, as if to herself: "Poor, poor Kord. He saw the unattainable and was shocked to find that he wanted it. He found himself lusting after white women! So he destroyed the images, hoping to destroy the desire itself."

Suddenly, she was laughing hysterically. Kymri slapped her and held her until, shivering, she became still.

Neither of them had heard the feet in the corridor. Neither of them knew they were no longer alone.

Until Urlanrey spoke. And as he spoke, Kymri and Mirlena were seized firmly by officers of the Pryterguard. Stasius also was present, inspecting the remains of Kord Vengel.

"My son," said Urlanrey to Kymri, "I look upon you with little pleasure. You know the penalty for this grievous act?"

"My father," said Kymri, looking at the man who was truly his father, "I know the price and am content to pay. The journey of my life has been short, but not without interest—according to the pleasure of Godfred."

"Lady Mirlena," went on the king coldly, "you and your companions received our hospitality. Is this how you repay?"

"We came here to seek the man who is now dead, not to insult you or your people. We had hoped to find him and bring him back before any harm could be done. We failed. I am sorry indeed that the king's law has been disobeyed and that offence has been given to the beliefs of you and your people. Most of all I am sorry that what has happened has brought us all to the brink of disaster."

"How is this so?"

Mirlena sighed wearily. "I think you will exercise your rights, and we shall have to die. Then I am afraid that my companions in the vessel in the sky will act not in justice but in vengeance. And they will do terrible things to your people and your beautiful city."

"That remains to pass. If, indeed, it comes to pass, it will be the pleasure of Godfred . . ." He looked at Kymri thoughtfully. "However, the king's son need not die. The blood royal has the right of entry into the Abode of the Dead . . . Is that not so, Stasius?"

The Lord of the Generators came to his monarch. "That is so, Urlanrey. And let all present know that Kymri op Kymriso is the acknowledged son of the king."

The officers of the Pryterguard took their hands from Kymri as if he had suddenly become red-hot.

Mirlena looked at him. "You did not tell me this."

"I did not know until a little time ago." Kymri took Mirlena's hand. "My father, this woman—though not of our race—is to me as my wife. As she fares, so let it fare with me. The sin belongs to us both. I am content to share its burden; but I will lift my hand against any who would separate me from the one I have chosen . . . My lord, I fear I have transgressed too greatly to remain the king's son. Nevertheless, I am proud of the blood that flows in me."

Urlanrey regarded his son intently. "Would you, then, voyage with this woman to her land across the sky?"

Kymri felt confused and foolish. All his brave words were noises in the air, nothing more. "It pleases the king to remind me that I am a fool. Yet I cannot unsay the words I have spoken."

"And would you, Lady Mirlena, remain to share the fate of this foolish young man whose spirit is great yet whose mind is ill-formed?"

"Urlanrey, I have learned to love and respect the young man you say is your son. What my companions would do if I tried to remain, I do not know. What you yourself will do, I do not know. It seems that whatever happens will end in disaster. But

179

before we are all committed to some course of action, the end of which can bring security to none, I would like to ask if you know what you call the Abode of the Dead really is?"

"The Abode of the Dead is where the ancient spirits of Noi Lantis dwell. Once it was inhabited by great ones whose knowledge of electrics, medicines and other mysteries far surpasses that of our wisest men. But the great ones displeased Godfred and were destroyed. All that remains are their metal servants and the secrets they guard. It is permitted that we should take and use only what we understand how to use. This much and no more."

"Have you heard the dead man speak—the one whose skin is as mine?"

It was Stasius who answered. "We have seen the man and heard his voice, but it was not fitting to linger in such a presence. The dead do not care to be disturbed."

Mirlena smiled wanly. "My lords, you are right and you are wrong. Kymri and I have heard the dead man's story. We have seen much of the Abode of the Dead, and its mystery is not difficult to understand.

"Two thousand years ago," went on Mirlena, "the forest did not exist. There was nothing but snow and ice and these underground halls where men and women skilled in electrics and many other things pursued their studies and work. With the war between the white races and the black, the cities of the Earth and the people remaining on Earth were destroyed. Except for these skilled men and women in their remote refuge in the icy wastes. But the war was of such fury that it changed not only the face of the Earth but the weather as well. At the same time, nature herself helped in the destruction by reducing Earth's magnetic field until it became nothing. Meanwhile, the men and women who lived here had children, grew old and died. And their children had children, and their children's children. And because there were so few of them, with each generation a little more learning was lost. During this time, the ice was melting, the forest was beginning to grow. In the end, the descendants of those who lived below the face of the Earth found that they could live on the surface of the Earth. They prospered and built the city of New Atlantis . . . Here, two thousand years ago, your own ancestors lived—they whom you call the great ones . . . There has been one dreadful war between the white races and the black Whatever you do, Urlanrey, try to avoid another."

Urlanrey gave her a thin smile. "One thing is certain, my daughter. You will not return to the world you call Mars." He turned to Kymri: "Soon, you shall stand with me, and I will listen to the dead man's story. It is my wish and my command . . . Now let us leave the sombre glories of the past and return to the sunlight."

"You do not intend to kill us?" asked Kymri.

"I intend to remind the Lady Mirlena of the story of the dragon the man and the condasnake."

Stasius said: "What shall be done with the dead one?"

Urlanrey sighed. "His problems end as ours begin. Let us leave him with what he found but did not seek . . . Is it not the task of the metal servants to cleanse and maintain the home of our fathers?"

Kord Vengel was left to silence, amid the debris and the enduring triumphs of a world that was lost in time.

CHAPTER THIRTY-THREE

Urlanrey, reflected Mirlena, was a surprising and enigmatic man. She suspected now that he had always known far more about the Martians, the state of Earth and the origins of his own people than he had pretended to know. She suspected that he and Stasius, both of them intelligent and oddly impenetrable men, had long been in possession of knowledge that they had judged it wise to conceal. Perhaps it was simply intuitive knowledge. Perhaps they realized that people, their people, were not ready to face much reality, and that truth should be revealed slowly. Or perhaps she credited them with too much wisdom. Perhaps they were simply cautious. She wondered if she would live long enough—and, if so, whether she would ever have enough evidence—to arrive at the truth.

The king, the Lord of the Generators, Kymri, Mirlena and the guards emerged from the Abode of the Dead in bright morning sunlight. Mirlena felt she could hardly walk. There was something more than the G force of Earth pulling her down: there was the oppressive burden of knowledge—and fear.

"Lady Mirlena," said the inscrutable Urlanrey, "you who were my guest are now both my guest and my prisoner. It would seem fitting that you return to your companions who yet live and acquaint them with the happenings of this night. On pain of death, none of you are to leave the Temple of Godfred . . . Now, I will dwell upon these events and upon your future. It has pleased Godfred that your presence should add greatly to the dangers that beset Noi Lantis." He turned to Kymri. "My son, you will attend me. There are matters on which I wish to be further informed. Also, perhaps you would care to justify the acts of one who has brought so much trouble in so short a space."

"My father, you have not forgotten the words that passed between us in the Abode of the Dead?"

"I have not forgotten."

"And the Lady Mirlena will live until we meet again?"

The king sighed. "Be content that I am aware of the difference between execution and assassination. Justice, unlike murder, must be seen if it is to succeed." He smiled grimly. "Perhaps these matters are arranged differently on the far world of Mars."

Mirlena said: "Urlanrey, whatever happens, I am already punished. I have given offence where I wished to give friendship. My companion who is dead has brought disaster not on himself alone. I will join my friends, as you wish, hoping that, whatever your decision is, it will be tempered by understanding . . ." She turned to make her way across the courtyard to the Hall of the King's Retreat.

Rudlan and Garl were waiting for her anxiously. She sank wearily on to her bed, and told them all that had happened.

"So Kord has dropped us in at the deep end," said Rudlan bitterly. "I always knew the man was programmed for destruction—his or somebody else's or both. In this case, the lot . . . If it hadn't been for those bloody Vaneyites back home, he would never have been chosen."

"It's futile to waste energy reviling Kord," said Mirlena. "He is—was—as Mars Vaneyism made him. Now we have to think hard and try to salvage something."

"We're on a no-win basis," said Garl gloomily. "I suppose we might just manage to avoid a general blood-bath if we can get the facts about Kord back to Mars. But if Urlanrey doesn't let you—and us—return to orbit, we are all sunk. Streven will get orders to turn this place into a glass skating rink."

"One thing is certain," said Rudlan. "We'll have to get all the news back to Streven quickly. The ship will be coming over the horizon pretty soon. The last time I should have made contact, those fool priests must have neutralized me with some kind of spark transmission. Either they need new brushes on their generators, or they have learned a bit about transformers and are playing about with voltage step-ups and spark gaps."

"Can you transmit from here?"

"I'd rather not. The loss of signal strength is high enough already, and the general background noises are frightful anyway . . . Don't you think they will let us use the courtyard? They didn't interfere before."

Mirlena shrugged. "None of us had violated their sacred shrine before. We can only try. If they turn us back, you'll have to do the best you can here."

But no one turned them back. Instead, oddly, they were completely ignored. When Rudlan had first used his transceiver in the temple courtyard, the priests had gathered like children round a new toy. This time, no one at all cast a glance in their direction.

It was as if, thought Mirlena, the three black Martians had suddenly become invisible. They were in the centre of the courtyard, less than fifty paces from the Abode of the Dead, and priests were walking from one part of the temple to another, engaged, no doubt, in their normal routines; but no one appeared to notice the three strangers, though one or two of the priests passed very close indeed.

It was an odd sensation. Crazily, Mirlena began to feel transparent, as if she had already become a ghost. Perhaps, now that they had offended Urlanrey, the visitors were tabu. Perhaps, even, they were tabu because they were already under sentence of death.

Neither Garl nor Rudlan appeared to be worried by the situation. Possibly they were not even aware of it—or, knowing that Mirlena was exhausted and depressed, they were concealing their reactions for her sake.

"Noi Lantis to orbit, Noi Lantis to orbit. Come in please."

Rudlan did not have to repeat his signals long before Streven Luse himself answered.

"Glad you could make contact," said Streven. "You had us worried when you failed last time. What happened?"

"Interference," said Rudlan briefly. "Streven we have news for you. It's not good, and you are not going to like it."

Captain Luse gave a grim laugh. "I have news for you, also not good. And as I am a coward, I'll unload mine first . . . Are you all there?"

"All except Kord. He's dead."

"That is your bad news, I suppose."

"Part of it. He left us with a horrible situation on our hands . . . Now, Captain, cheer us up with your small item."

"I will—and I'll enter my cowardice in the log . . . We've lost the sloop. We have also lost Meiron Menders and three others. But we have lost the sloop . . . Mirlena, Garl, Rudlan, that is the tragedy you are going to have to live with for some time, if you can . . . Do you understand what I mean?"

The three Martians looked at each other, their faces frozen, mask-like. There was a silence. They could think of nothing to say.

"Are you receiving me? Are you receiving me?"

Rudlan Others gave a bitter smile. "Yes, Streven, we are receiving you. I wish we were not . . . But—but the ship is designed for planetary touch-down. Surely something can be managed?"

"Listen, all of you." There was a break in Streven Luse's voice. "It is true that the ship can touch down. But you know what the vessel's mass is, and touch-down would have to be under virtually ideal conditions on an absolutely stable geological base. Eight people remain on board, plus the samples and masses of data we have already acquired. I hate to remind you what this expedition has already cost Mars. What I have to say—

and I wish, I wish I could avoid it—is that, as Captain, I cannot hazard the vessel and the remaining crew. Physically, and as far as a vessel of this kind is concerned, the conditions within thousands of kilometres of Noi Lantis are disastrous . . . Mirlena, Rudlan, Garl, forgive me. Please forgive me. I shall have to abandon you."

It was Mirlena who answered him. "Streven, the news has shattered us, but there is nothing to forgive. We understand that you can't gamble everything . . . What is your programme now?"

"I propose to remain in orbit until we have settled what your plans and prospects are on the surface. Then I shall shoot for Mars as fast as this damned can will go. I shall call them to have another sloop ready and try to persuade them to authorize a fast turn-around. But, Mirlena, you know the facts of life. It is going to be a long time before turn-around, even if the government gives top priority, regardless of cost. You know also that both journeys are going to be longer because we came at the most favourable time. Now, Mars and Earth are many more millions of miles away from each other."

"I don't think you need worry too much about the time factor," said Mirlena. "If we survive the next few days, we shall probably be able to survive months, perhaps even years." And then she told him all that had happened.

"I see," said Streven Luse, when she had finished. "Well there is at least one answer to that. I'll stay in orbit for ten more days. If Rudlan doesn't make contact regularly, I'll raze Noi Lantis to the ground . . . Perhaps this Urlanrey would appreciate a demonstration of force. Shall I flatten a few thousand square kilometres of forest?"

"No!" snapped Mirlena. "Streven, don't think like Kord. Please don't think like Kord . . . We are the intruders here. These people lived in peace before we came along. The one thing that horrifies me is that all those damned Vaneyites on Mars will work themselves up into a blood-lust when they hear of this little tragedy . . . Don't let them send you back with orders to kill, Streven. Wreck the ship first."

"I knew I had one tiny bit of good news to tell you," said Streven Luse, "but I don't suppose it will mean as much now as it might have done. Hard Vaneyism is on the way out. Kastril tried to shoot the President, and got killed himself . . . So I don't think the fanatics who are left will have enough power to impose their policies any more. With Kastril, it was a one-man show."

"If I were not so miserable," said Mirlena, "and so damned tired, I'd dance for joy—even under Earth G."

"Listen, Streven," said Rudlan excitedly, "the contact is going. You're getting near the horizon. But we'll talk some more next time round—I hope. And it has just occurred to me that, if we live, there are enough materials here to build a very powerful transmitter . . . It seems I shall have plenty of time. That way, we can re-establish contact with you on the way back. Dammit, given time, I might devise something powerful enough to reach Mars itself."

Streven Luse's voice was beginning to crackle and quiver as the vessel passed out of range. "What are you going to do with yourselves—if you live?"

It was Mirlena who answered that one. "We could always start a university," she said, in a futile attempt to be light-hearted.

There was no means of knowing if Streven Luse had heard her.

Rudlan collapsed the transceiver aerial. The three Martians looked bleakly at each other.

"Let us all go into the Abode of the Dead and sing rude songs," said Garl drily, "then we can help Urlanrey to make up his mind to do us all a big favour."

"Mirlena," said Rudlan, "that crack about a university wasn't very funny."

"I know."

"That's not what I mean. If they let us live . . . *If* they let us live, we shall have to do something. Besides, these damned priests are so stupid about their electrics, it bothers me."

Mirlena tried to smile. "Rudlan, I've known you all this time,

187

and I never suspected you were an idealist . . . What a rotten psychologist I am." Then she saw Kymri walking towards them across the courtyard.

"From Urlanrey to the guests of Urlanrey, greetings," he said formally. Then a smile broke over his face. "Mirlena, my father bids me remind you that the wise man did nothing."

"What the Vaney does that mean?" demanded Garl.

"It means," said Mirlena, in Martian, "that Urlanrey has more wisdom than any of us. All we have is knowledge. Perhaps Rudlan is right. Perhaps we should offer an exchange."

Then she told Kymri of all that had passed between the Martians on Earth and Streven Luse in orbit.

Kymri looked at the three of them. "I am sorry," he said, "that you are far from your own world. But I believe that you who are skilled in electrics and other profound mysteries will find a way to talk to your own people. I believe also that, as you say, they will return to see how you fare among the white savages."

Suddenly, surprisingly, he began to laugh. "Such is the humour of Godfred," he said.

And suddenly, crazily, infectiously, the four of them were laughing. Three black Martians and a white man of Earth.

After the destruction of a satellite and the devastation of a planet, after the death of a civilization and of countless millions of people, after two thousand years of hatred on Mars, and after long centuries of isolation and ignorance on the last living continent of Earth, the colour of human skin seemed to be of less importance than the spirit which moved it.

Such was the humour of Godfred.

Kymri sat in his customary chair in the radio and tracking station on top of the tower of the Halls of Inheritance. Once the structure had been known as the Abode of the Dead. He was savouring a moment that was wonderful and would belong to him for ever. He had found the Martian vessels. Rough calculations showed that they were about half a million kilometres out and coming in·at some fifty thousand kilometres an hour on a course that should bring them tangentially to Earth.

Kymri looked down through the observation window at the courtyard of the Temple of Godfred. Rudlan was demonstrating his favourite toy, his radio-telescope, to priest-students. The dish telescope had picked up the Martian Expedition almost as soon as it had lifted clear of Mars. But that was not the same thing. Anyone could have tracked the vessels with that kind of equipment.

It was a warm, sunny afternoon. The sky was clear—a rarity for the rain forests of Antarctica. Farther away in the courtyard, Garl was teaching atomic theory to half a dozen advanced students. Garl claimed he had found a couple of geniuses—natural physicists. Maybe he was right. But Garl was a fellow o great enthusiasms.

Mirlena was nowhere to be seen. No doubt the heat was too much for her. Perhaps she was closeted with Kymriso in the coo chambers of the palace—those two were very close and secretive these days—or perhaps she was simply resting. She had the clini as well as her lectures and demonstrations. She was going to have to give something up.

Absently, Kymri's fingers had been twiddling the dials on the panel in front of him. Suddenly, the words came out of the speaker like thunderbolts.

"Space Ship Timon Harland to Noi Lantis. Do you read me? Space Ship Timon Harland to Noi Lantis. Do you read me?"

Kymri had not expected plain language contact so soon. Bu then the sky was clear, and it must have amused Godfred to kil all the electric storms in Antarctica.

"New Atlantis to Timon Harland. New Atlantis to Timon Harland. I read you. Welcome," said Kymri in fluent Martian.

"Timon Harland to Noi—New Atlantis. Streven Luse, Commodore, here. To whom am I speaking?"

"Kymri op Kymriso—the white savage . . . Greetings, Streven. It has been a long time."

"Kymri! How—how are you?"

"I am well, Mirlena is well, Rudlan and Garl are well. I estimate you to be half a million kilometres out, with a speed of fifty thousand kilometres an hour. It looks from here as if you will try for the two-hour orbit. Am I correct?"

"Yes, but . . . Man alive, Kymri. You have me dazed."

Kymri was enjoying himself. He heard a clang somewhere down the tower, but took no notice of it. "Your ship is called the Timon Harland. I appreciate the significance. What are the names of your other two vessels?"

"The Meiron Menders and the Urlanrey."

"You have chosen good names . . . Tell me, Streven, why did the first vessel not have a name?"

Streven Luse laughed. "I expect you know your Martian

politics by now. Gondomar Kastril wanted the President to name it Gondomar Kastril. But the President wouldn't. So Kastril said it would have no name, and the President said that was all right, because then everyone would know that it belonged to the people."

"Then why name these vessels? They, too, belong to the people."

"So do the illustrious names they bear. Kymri, we have brought you a great cargo."

"What kind of things?"

"Medical supplies, text-books, printing presses, transistors, cathode ray tubes, earth-moving equipment, a computer, cement mixers, an electron microscope, blue-prints and detailed plans of every known mechanical device—you name it, we have it. Also we have brought scientists, technicians, teachers and even, I am afraid, an ambassador."

"This must have cost the people of Mars a great deal." Kymri felt a hand on his shoulders, and looked round to see Mirlena standing behind him.

"Not too much," responded Streven Luse happily. "We disbanded Kastril's security police and cut the civil service in half to pay for it."

"Have you brought a good obstetrician?" asked Kymri.

"Have we brought what?"

"A gynaecologist," explained Kymri. He took Mirlena's hand and held it. "My wife, a Martian, has endured three and a half years of Earth gravity. She has endured it well, but I do not care to see her face the additional stress of childbirth under such conditions. It occurred to me that, if you are agreeable, she could be delivered in orbit."

"Kymri, we will look after Mirlena and her baby as if—as if they were the most important people in the world."

"Perhaps they are," said Kymri. "The baby is the first child of two worlds . . . Incidentally, when you touch down, Streven, you must allow me to show you the Shrine of the Unknown Negro. It is a very moving experience."

"So I have heard . . . But do there have to be negroes and

white men any more?"

"We here are cultivating a disease called colour-blindness. [
shows promising results . . . I'll cut out now, Streven. I hav
a lot of news to give my people. By the way, I taped our con
versation. With your permission, I propose to replay it over th
New Atlantis Broadcasting System—with translation for thos
who do not yet speak Martian, of course."

"Kymri, words fail me. I can only say that we will see yo
very soon—and we can hardly wait."

"We, too, are somewhat overcome. I'll resume contact in on
hour. Over and out."

Mirlena looked at Kymri. Her hair was white—perhap
bleached by the strange climate or by the stresses of Eart
gravity, or both—but to Kymri she was no less beautiful.

Suddenly, she remembered a moment they had shared thre
and a half years before. A moment they had shared with a dea
man whose words had survived him.

"They are coming to help us rebuild the temple," she sai
softly, unaware of the rivulets on her cheeks.

Kymri stood up and held her gently, his body alive to th
swelling within hers and to the mysterious movements of life

"They are coming to reclaim the last continent with us," h
said, stroking the stiff white hair. "Not Antarctica. I have onl
just realized what it is. The last continent is man."

Outside the tower, a refreshing breeze rippled across the lat
afternoon. And somewhere, perhaps for a man long dead, ;
wild bird was singing.

*For regular early information about forthcoming novels
send a postcard giving your name and address in block
capitals to Mrs. Jean Povey, Hodder and Stoughton Ltd.,
St. Paul's House, Warwick Lane, London, E.C.4.*